MOBBED UP

King Rio

Lock Down Publications and Ca$h Presents

Mobbed Up

A Novel by *King Rio*

King Rio

Lock Down Publications
P.O. Box 944
Stockbridge, Ga 30281
www.lockdownpublications.com

Copyright 2021 by King Rio
Mobbed Up

Lock Down Publications
Like our page on Facebook: Lock Down Publications @
www.facebook.com/lockdownpublications.ldp
Book interior design by: **Shawn Walker**
Edited by: **Jill Alicea**

Stay Connected with Us!

Text **LOCKDOWN** to 22828 to stay up-to-date with new releases, sneak peaks, contests and more...
Thank you!

Submission Guideline.

Submit the first three chapters of your completed manuscript to ldpsubmissions@gmail.com, subject line: Your book's title. The manuscript must be in a .doc file and sent as an attachment. Document should be in Times New Roman, double spaced and in size 12 font. Also, provide your synopsis and full contact information. If sending multiple submissions, they must each be in a separate email.

Have a story but no way to send it electronically? You can still submit to LDP/Ca$h Presents. Send in the first three chapters, written or typed, of your completed manuscript to:

LDP: Submissions Dept
P.O. Box 944
Stockbridge, Ga 30281

DO NOT send original manuscript. Must be a duplicate.

Provide your synopsis and a cover letter containing your full contact information.

Thanks for considering LDP and Ca$h Presents.

Mobbed Up

PROLOGUE

"Damn, look at shorty," D-Lo said, looking up from his smartphone.

The girl was very short and very pretty, reddish-brown in complexion, with an erotically sexy smile and a fat round ass to go with it. The friend crossing the street with her was taller (though not by much), thicker, just as pretty, and roughly the same complexion.

Stone-faced, Jah watched them approach, not knowing their identities, but knowing almost for certain their reason for walking up. For the past hour or so, he and his best friend D-Lo - both seventeen-year-old Traveling Vice Lords - had been posted up across the street from a house party on the 1600 block of Millard Avenue, leaning back against the passenger's side of D-Lo's dark blue Dodge Challenger R/T and listening to the music quaking from the Challenger's trunk while the two of them smoked blunts and sold Molly to the partygoers.

The two girls were dressed almost identically. Their white tube tops were exposed by their open red leather jackets, their leggings snug and colorful, their '95 Nike Air Max sneakers a shade darker than the jackets.

"One of y'all named Jah?" the shorter girl asked.

"Yeah, what's up?" Jah said.

Her smile widened. "I'm Camri, and this my sister Nai'yonna. We heard you got that good Molly on deck. How much for two of 'em?"

"I need a dub for every pill."

"Nah, hold up," D-Lo said. He dug in the right-hand pocket of his fur-lined, blue leather Pelle Pelle coat and withdrew his own bag of Molly. He handed Camri two pills.

"How much?" she asked.

"Gimme thirty and yo' phone number and we'll call it even. Where y'all from?"

Jah shook his head, thinking, *This nigga just as tender as my big brother with these bitches.* Looking away, Jah spotted an older man moving aggressively in his direction. The man had just stormed out of the party across the street, his expression dark with animosity.

"Ay, li'l nigga!" the man shouted.

Camri turned and gasped. "Aw, shit," she said, taking a step back. "Sharon told him y'all been out here servin' on his block. I was just about to tell y'all that."

Two other guys, both of whom Jah recognized as CVLs from down this way, departed from the crowded sidewalk and fell in step beside the older man.

"Bruh," Jah said, suddenly wishing he hadn't left his Glock handgun under the passenger's seat. "I'm about to drop this nigga soon as he get up close."

"On Neal," D-Lo agreed.

One of the guys walking with the older man said, "Stain, chill out. Let me talk to these—"

"Hell nah!" Stain shot back. "Li'l niggas got me fucked up."

He was closing in: seven feet away, five feet, three...

Jah threw a punch, his long right arm extending rapidly, like a venomous snake lashing out to sink its poison-dripping teeth into the warm-blooded flesh of unsuspecting prey, only instead of fangs, there were Jah's bony knuckles, colliding with Stain's mouth and sending the man stumbling backward. Jah followed up with a left that struck the side of Stain's face and another right that hit the man's rock-hard forehead just as someone else's fist - one of the guys who'd accompanied Stain across the street - rocked his own forehead.

He heard Camri yell, "Martez, let them fight!"

But there was no time to register the blind-sider's name, because just then Stain rushed forward - all six-foot, two-hundred-some pounds of him - and clamped his powerful arms around Jah's waist. He had Jah in the air a second later, and slammed down onto the hood of the Challenger a second after that.

In the split-second Jah was airborne, he looked over and saw that Stain's two accomplices were jumping D-Lo, punching and kneeing him against the side of the sports car.

"Beat his ass, daddy!" a girl shouted from the growing crowd that was now spilling out of the party and into the street.

Jah twisted and wrestled his way out of Stain's arms and landed four more hard punches to the graying stubble on the man's face before he was grabbed and head-butted on the mouth and slammed again, this time to the pavement.

Jah's right shoulder hit the ground hard. The back of his right hand hit the ground even harder. The bag of Molly pills in the right-hand pocket somehow busted open and went bouncing across the pavement in every direction, along with all the cash he had in his pocket.

"You done, li'l nigga? Huh?" Stain's breath was hot and stinky in Jah's face.

"Yeah, man," Jah said, realizing that Stain was already out of breath and ready to call it quits.

Stain squeezed Jah as tightly as he could, showing his strength in hopes of dissuading the youngster from trying for any more punches, then let go and scooted away before standing up. Jah got up, saw that that D-Lo was still down, and went to help his homie up off the ground.

"Get the fuck from over here!" Stain said.

Jah looked at their faces, memorizing them for a later time. One guy — a fat black dude Jah hadn't seen until now — had a gun in his hand and was standing next to Stain. He pointed the gun at Jah and said nothing.

Jah helped D-Lo into the passenger's seat, then went around to the driver's side, got in, and burned rubber as he sped off down Millard Avenue.

"You still got that K in the trunk?" Jah asked as he rounded the corner onto 16th Street.

D-Lo looked over at Jah and nodded his head, wiping blood from his mouth and nose as some new Memphis rapper named Moneybagg Yo's latest mixtape throbbed from the speakers.

"Turn around," D-Lo said.

"You already know," Jah said.

King Rio

Chapter 1

Sincere Owens was nicknamed "Rell" because his middle name was Jerrell. His pops, David "Big Man" Owens, had started calling him Rell when he was a child, and the name stuck with the people on 13th and Avers where he was born and raised by his mother, Maria, after Big Man left her for Susan when she was pregnant with Jah, Rell's younger brother.

Here lately he and Pops were getting along better, making up for lost time. Last weekend they'd gone to a Bears game together, which is where Rell had gotten the sweatshirt. He had a hat to go with it, but he'd left it in his car with all the other items he planned to bring up to the apartment once his father and stepmother were gone.

Big Man was indeed a big man: 6'6", 280 pounds with a bunch of muscle underneath the fat. Rell thought his pops dressed like an ex-pimp. He was always wearing a bright-colored suit with gator skin shoes and a top hat, and maybe a fur coat, all of which he was wearing now as he lugged his luggage down the stairs.

But at the moment, Rell wasn't thinking about his father's obnoxious wardrobe. The pretty girl who'd just shut the door in his face had his full attention.

"Don't be partying in my place," Big Man said as he passed behind Rell. "Take your friends somewhere else if you wanna have some fun. Just make sure you keep watch on the apartment. Got a lot of valuable stuff in there. These niggas 'round here will rob you before you can blink."

The door in front of Rell opened again as Big Man was making his way down the stairs. This time it was a different girl, just as pretty-faced but lighter, and this time the door opened up all the way.

"Come on in," she said, stepping aside for him. "I'm Tirzah. Tamera's getting the money ready now."

"That's her name?" he asked. "The one who looked out first?"

"Yeah. She's my sister."

"Is she single?" The question fell out of Rell's mouth almost unintentionally.

Tirzah smiled and put a thumbnail between her teeth. She had cute little dimples in her cheeks, just like Tamera. Rell couldn't help but notice that Tirzah was wearing a small pair of boy shorts as he walked in.

"I'm sorry," he said as she led him to a sofa. "Didn't mean nothing by that - if she got a man, I mean. I'm respectful. I just...I don't know."

Tirzah put a hand on her hip and kept right on smiling, still biting down on the thumbnail.

Then Tamera walked in from the hallway that Rell knew led to the two bedrooms, and suddenly Rell no longer noticed Tirzah.

His eyes scanned Tamera from bottom to top, from her clean white socks with the sky blue toes and heels, to the tiny pair of blue and gray boy shorts that left her luscious chocolate thighs exposed, to the small white T-shirt with a picture of Gucci Mane in a Santa Claus outfit in the center of it, and finally to her stunning brown visage. Her hair, short and jet black, looked like it had recently been professionally done. It was straight and parted down the middle.

She had the prettiest face, one of those memorable faces that would have Rell daydreaming about her forever and a day. She took the same pose as her sister, but the way Tamera's legs were formed made for a mouthwatering stance. She was "pigeon-toed", as most people called it.

What Rell could not keep his eyes off was the plump print in the crotch of her shorts. He felt compelled to give that exact spot a long, hard kiss, and a whole lot more.

"What's your name again?" Tamera asked him.

Tirzah cut in, "He asked me if you had a man."

"Damn. Snitchin'-ass girl," Rell said.

Both of the girls laughed.

"My name's Rell. Well, Sincere, but everybody calls me Rell. Big Man is my pops."

Tamera walked over to the table and bent over to pick up some cash that was laying on the lid of an open pizza box. Then she went in a purse that stood next to the box and took out $90 more.

He got up as she gave him the rent money. "Thanks. Y'all have a Merry Christmas. I'll be upstairs if y'all need anything."

Tamera wasn't letting him off the hook. "Where are you from? How come I've never seen you over here if Big Man's your daddy?"

"I do me." Rell chuckled, grinning at the beautiful brown girl. "You are so fuckin' sexy. I'm sorry, just telling the truth. Much love. Y'all have a blessed day."

"Thanks, sweetie." Tamera blushed as she and Tirzah followed Rell to the door.

Rell had to go and collect the rest of the rent from the building's other tenants – well, from all but one tenant. The woman on the first floor, some woman Pops had described as "the big-mouthed girl with the big ol' titties", was refusing to pay rent until the first of January, which was fine with Big Man, but she wouldn't be getting the $75 shaved off her rent like the others.

Rell was just glad to be getting the rent money for himself. Pops was letting him keep this month's rent from all the tenants for staying two weeks at the apartment while Big Man and Susan vacationed in Miami.

He turned to say a final word to the girls as he stepped out into the snow-tracked hallway.

Tamera had her bottom lip tucked behind her upper teeth, wearing an expression so obviously seductive that Rell opened his mouth and didn't say a word.

"See you later, Rell," Tirzah said and then shut the door of apartment 4B.

Rell went on to collect rent from seven more apartments and was more than happy to pocket the entire $6,000. Then he helped Pops load the luggage into Susan's SUV and waved at them as they drove off down Douglas.

He turned and looked up at the yellow brick apartment building. It was freezing cold out, and snow was everywhere — packed onto the windows, piled high at the curbs, salted down on the sidewalk. Five young boys were standing on the corner, bundled up in heavy coats and hoodies, smoke from their warm breaths billowing out of their mouths as they talked.

Rell was ducking into his car — the white 2013 Impala Pops had gotten him when he came home from prison just two years ago — when he happened to glance at the fourth floor windows. Tamera and Tirzah were at one of the windows, gazing down at him. They waved excitedly.

Rell's grin broadened.

He took a quarter-ounce of OG Kush and a subcompact .40-caliber Glock pistol out of his glove compartment and dropped them in his back pockets before setting the car alarm and heading inside.

Tamera's pretty face never left his mind.

Chapter 2

Big Man had impeccable taste in furniture. Big black leather sofas and intricately carved end tables sat atop the living room's spotless hardwood floor, and the 65" TV was perfect for all the football games Rell planned to watch over the next two weeks.

He got a Budweiser from the fridge and a package of microwavable hot wings from the freezer, then riffled through the kitchen cabinets until the wings were done. There was a lot of food, good stuff that Rell loved to eat. He wondered if Pops would be upset to come home to a bunch of empty cabinets.

He sat down at the kitchen table and dialed his mother's phone number on his smartphone, setting it next to his plate on speakerphone so that he could talk and eat at the same time.

"You at Big Man's?" Maria asked.

As usual, Rell could hear the loud television in the background. Momma always had the volume on 100.

"Yeah, he just left with Susan," Rell said.

"That bitch."

"Don't call her that, Ma." Rell chuckled. "Stop bein' mean."

"Your brother just made it in. He got jumped on at some party last night, and one of his friends got killed. You really need to sit down and have a talk with this boy since his daddy won't. He's going down the same path you went down. Sooner or later his ass is gonna be locked up, too."

"He got jumped?" Rell frowned.

"Yeah, he got jumped. Ain't that what the hell I just said? You deaf?"

"Put him on the phone."

"He's asleep."

"Well, wake him up."

"Boy, I am watching TV. Call his damn phone. He'll wake up and answer it. And I know ya daddy paid you good to stay over there. I need some money. You know I just spent all that money on Jah and that baby of his for Christmas. I'm broke, Rell. Barely even got enough to pay my rent."

Rell chuckled and shook his head. Momma was always asking for money. She was an anesthesiologist at Northwestern Memorial Hospital, making more than enough to pay her bills and then some, but she never went a day without complaining about money.

"I might have a few hundred for you." Rell sucked all the meat off a hot wing and took a swig of the beer. "Let me call Jah. I'll call you back."

"Make sure you call Erica, too. She came by looking for you this morning."

"Yup. I'll call her."

"Good. And don't call me back until at least 3:30. I'm watching my shows."

Rell could only shake his head as he cleaned off his greasy fingers with a napkin and ended the call.

Momma was something else.

Rell was 22 years old, and Jahlil was 17, the same age Rell had been when he was arrested and sentenced to five years in prison for an assault and armed home invasion back in 2010. Erica, his girlfriend at the time, had cheated on him with a guy he'd gone to high school with, and when he showed up and kicked in the door of Erica's apartment, she had already called the police. The cops showed up as he was pistol-whipping the guy and arrested him on the spot. He'd been released after serving just three out of the five years, because he'd gotten his GED and a few more time cuts during his prison bid.

x

He was just about to dial Jah's number when the house phone rang. There was one cordless phone on the wall next to the refrigerator and another one in the living room. He ignored the house phone and dialed Jah's number on his smartphone. He would call back whoever had called the house phone, but the situation with Jah took precedence over everything.

As Momma had said he would, Jah answered the phone, sounding groggy and out of it.

"'Sup, big bruh. Shit. What time is it?"

"Time for you to get the fuck up and tell me what went down last night."

"Is Pops gone already?"

"Yeah, he just left."

"Damn. I wanted to ask him for some money."

"You sound like Momma." Rell bit into another wing. "You got beat up?"

"Man, hell yeah. Some grown-ass nigga pieced me up. Think he one of the older guys from off Millard. He got mad 'cause I knocked out his punk-ass guy. I had a couple of the guys wit' me. We came back blowin'. I had that K. Li'l bro D-Lo had a pole, too, but shit, he got popped up soon as we slid down on them niggas. They hit him in the face. We had to leave him out there. Man, I'm ready to go back over there, bruh. They took D-Lo; I'm takin' one of them."

Rell shook his head. "Come over here to Pops' spot with me."

"I ain't lettin' that shit—"

"Just come over here, li'l bruh. I ain't tryna hear that shit. You shouldn't have been over there in the first place."

"I'm grown as fuck, nigga. I go where the fuck I wanna go."

"If you want this money I got for you and Momma, you gon' bring your ass over here. Get dressed. Hurry up." Rell ended the call abruptly because he knew Jah would argue and he wasn't trying to hear it.

This was serious. Someone had been murdered, and Jah was involved. As much as Rell liked having a younger brother who took after him, he hated seeing Jah get caught up in all the gangbanging and gunplay. He wanted Jah to straighten up like he had over the past few years, especially now that their father had gotten rid of his heroin habit. Growing up in the North Lawndale neighborhood, Rell and Jah had been forced to take care of themselves for the most part. Momma helped out a little, but not much. She, too, had habits, though her choice of escape was prescription pills, weed, and alcohol. Big Man got sober a year before Rell went to prison and ended up going into real estate with Susan. Today the couple owned three west side duplex houses that they rented out and the apartment building, their biggest source of income. Big Man and Susan spent a lot of their profits on furs and jewelry, but Rell was almost certain that they had a nice amount of money saved up in their bank accounts. Every now and then Pops would give Rell a few hundred dollars, but this was the first time he'd gotten a large sum of money from the tight old man.

He waited until he was done eating to go to the wall-mounted phone. He checked the caller ID and saw the name T. Lyon.

The phone hardly rang once before it was picked up.

"Hello? Somebody called?" he said, leaning back against the stainless steel refrigerator and finishing off the beer.

"We, uhhh...the power just went out on us. I'm so sorry, do you mind coming back down to take a look when you get a chance?"

Rell grinned and shook his head, tossing the empty Budweiser bottle in the trash can. The voice belonged to Tamera.

He couldn't wait to get to apartment 4B and see her.

Chapter 3

"Why'd you do this? You are one big dummy, you know that?" Tamera couldn't believe it. She was standing with her hands on her hips, looking at all the cords Tirzah had plugged into every power socket in their kitchen.

Now the power was out.

"Hey, you're the one who wanted to see the nigga again. All I did was make it happen," Tirzah said, opening the blinds to let the sun in.

"This is not what I meant. It's the end of December in Chicago, way too damned cold to be playing with the electricity."

Tamera crossed her arms over her chest and sighed. She had an electric stove; the second box of pizza she'd put in the oven to warm up would have to wait.

"No need in pouting now." Tirzah was at the counter next to the sink, rolling a blunt. As always, she left the cigar tobacco scattered all across the counter. "I'll tell you one thing, sis. If Lil Webb was as fine as Rell, I would be married by now. Hell, I'd propose to Rell myself if he wasn't so focused on you."

"I wonder if he got any kids," Tamera said as she cracked open another Mountain Dew. "I know he didn't have a ring on. That's the first thing I looked at."

"Your thirsty ass would look for a ring first." Tirzah laughed as she sealed the blunt closed with a swipe of her tongue. "So, what did he say? Is he on his way down here?"

Tamera nodded and stared at her smartphone. It was still on Big Man's number. "He said give him a minute."

"He needs to hurry up. It's getting cold in here."

"We wouldn't be getting cold if you hadn't blown out the power. Jackass."

Tirzah smiled as she put fire to the blunt. "He's crushing Kendrick in the looks department. Looked like he had some muscles under that hoodie, too."

"It most definitely did."

"What if that nigga came in here and got naked right in front of us? What would you do?"

Tamera regarded her sister with the are-you-crazy look. "What do you think I'd do?"

Tirzah rolled her eyes and headed to the living room. Tamera followed her, thinking about Rell and the hunger she'd seen in his eyes as he gawked at her boy shorts. She could tell that he wanted her just as badly as she wanted him.

"You ain't about that life," Tirzah said as she plopped down Indian-style on the sofa. "Kendrick gon' fuck you up if he get word of you fuckin' around on him."

"Fuck Kendrick. That nigga had two kids on me. He's lucky I never cheated on his ass when he was home, and he's a real fool if he thinks I'm about to be faithful now. I'm single as a one-dollar bill."

"And Kendrick gon' make four quarters out of yo' ass." Tirzah busted out laughing, choking on the weed smoke at the same time.

Tamera rolled her eyes as she smiled and thought about Rell. She liked his style, from the way he dressed to his strong baritone voice. An image of him standing nude in front of her crossed Tamera's mind, causing her smile to widen.

Just then, there was a knock at the door. Three sharp thumps.

Tamera's eyes lit up, and she gasped.

She remembered the knock. In fact, she'd always remember the knock. It was the knock of the man she hoped was single and could be her knight in shining armor, someone to patch up her wounded heart and treat her like the queen she knew she was.

As she went to the door, she shook away the thoughts of him being all that she'd just imagined him to be. Men were dogs. More than likely, Rell was no different from the rest of the pack.

King Rio

Chapter 4

Rell was worried about his little brother and the drama Jah had gotten into last night, but the troubling thoughts seemed to evaporate when Tamera opened the door. His smile was as wide as hers.

"Y'all plottin' on me down here?" he said, walking in. "How the power cut off all of a sudden? That shit was just fine a few minutes ago."

Tamera sucked her teeth and shut the door behind him. "Are you here to question us or help? Big Man never complains."

"Yeah, well, I ain't Big Man."

The apartment wasn't that large. It only took Rell a few seconds to make it to the electrical panel in the hallway next to the bathroom door.

Tamera dipped into a bedroom and returned wearing a pair of black sweatpants just as Rell was resetting the power.

The lights came on. A cacophony of mechanical noises sounded from the kitchen. Frowning, Rell trailed Tamera to the kitchen, ogling the goodness she had going on behind her.

Tirzah beat them to the kitchen, but she wasn't fast enough. Rell got a chance to see the blender going with nothing in it, and the glass plate in the microwave rotating with nothing on it, and the bag on the vacuum cleaner that was laying on the white tiled floor swell up as it took in nothing but air.

Tamera and Tirzah rushed around the small kitchen, snatching out plugs and turning things off.

Meanwhile, Rell stood in silence and chuckled to himself. He knew exactly what had happened here.

"Y'all a trip," he said when the noise settled down.

Tamera pointed at Tirzah.

"Bitch, don't point at me!" Tirzah said, wearing the guiltiest expression.

"Both of y'all some snitches," Rell said.

Tamera gave him two middle fingers for the remark and then snatched the blunt from her sister. Rell sat down at the table and straightened a pepper shaker that had been knocked over in the sisters' haste to unplug everything.

"Let me hit that trash," he said, reaching for the blunt.

"Trash?" Tirzah said it as if he'd called her a bitch.

"Nigga, please. Gas what we smoke, nigga."

"A'ight, Sosa," Rell said with a chuckle. Looking from Tirzah to Tamera, he wondered how he'd missed seeing them in the past. He was from this neighborhood, had spent just about every day of his life in and around North Lawndale.

He asked Tamera where she and her sister were originally from. Tirzah answered for her.

"Shit, right here," Tirzah said. "In this same li'l bitty ass apartment. We done been here through three different landlords. Before Big Man it was Keith's fat, funky, nasty ass. Then, when we was little, it was Sherri. She died, I think."

"She did," Tamera confirmed. "Keith was her grandson. He sold the building to Big Man."

"Why yo' daddy think he a pimp?" Tirzah asked.

The question sent them all into a raucous laughter. Rell couldn't count the number of laughs he'd experienced at the expense of his father's ridiculous outfits. Most of his old friends on Avers had secretly changed Big Man's nickname to Pimpin' Dave, or Pimpin' Pimpin'. There were a number of other colorful names to describe Big Man's colorful wardrobe. Rell used to be embarrassed by his father's dress code, but now he only found it mildly amusing.

"Why I ain't never seen y'all around here before?" he asked, passing the blunt to Tirzah. "What, y'all niggas couldn't come outside or somethin'?"

"For what? To get shot?" Tamera shook her head. "I'm trying to live, you hear me? I really wanna get the fuck away from Chicago. Soon as I get my money right, I'm gone. Ain't shit out here but drama. Drama, drama, and more drama. Bitches fuckin' every nigga in the city and talkin' down on the next bitch. Niggas shootin' niggas over bullshit. This is not the place for me. If I do end up staying, I'm leaving the hood. Might move my ass out to Lincoln Park somewhere. It's nice out there."

"Yeah, I feel you," Rell said. He, too, was fed up with all the senseless violence. He didn't mention it, but he'd also been thinking of moving to a better area. Now that he was finally off parole and house arrest, he wanted to make sure he stayed away from the environment that had landed him in prison in the first place.

He took the sack of loud-scented high-grade marijuana and a cigarillo out of his pocket and rolled a blunt while Tirzah went on talking about her and Tamera's childhood. He learned that their stepfather — the man who helped raised them as children — had been shot and killed when they were in elementary school, and that their mom had met a guy on Facebook two years ago and moved to Boykins, Virginia to be with him, and that three months ago, Tirzah had lost her job at Pizza Hut for allegedly stealing money from the cash register. Tirzah blamed it on a coworker. Tamera said Tirzah's thieving ass had probably done it.

Rell didn't give a damn either way.

All he wanted was Tamera.

When she finally got around to asking him about his girlfriend, he was tempted to lie. Erica wasn't really what one would call a girlfriend. If anything, she was just a thot who he happened to be currently fucking, and he knew from past experiences that he wasn't the only one fucking her.

"I wouldn't call her a girlfriend," he said, lighting another blunt. "I'll put it like this: I fuck her, but I got to wear a condom every time."

"Oh. She's one of those." Tamera shook her head.

"Yeah. She done fucked everybody I know. I think my li'l brother might've even hit."

"Nasty hoe," Tirzah said.

Rell waved it off. He didn't really care much about Erica. He was just used to her. After getting out of prison, he'd spent twelve months on house arrest. Aside from going to work every weekday at a local bakery, he'd been in Momma's house every day, playing video games and watching sports games with Jah, and since Erica lived right around the corner, he had gone back to occasionally fucking her whenever the mood struck him.

His smartphone rang as he was passing the blunt to Tamera. It was Jah calling. Rell took the opportunity to discreetly gaze at Tamera's ass as he answered the call.

"I'm outside, bruh," Jah said. "Buzz me in. And you gotta pay this petty-ass nigga Bam a sawbuck. I told him you had it for bringing me."

Rell laughed as he got up. "On my way down there now." He hit end and chucked up the deuces to Tamera and Tirzah. "Catch y'all later. My li'l bruh downstairs. Don't fuck around and blow up the building. Next time just call up there and ask me to come down when y'all nosy mu'fuckas wanna know some shit."

Tamera rolled her eyes — to Rell, it was the sexiest eye-roll he'd ever seen — and Tirzah sucked her teeth. They followed him to the door.

"Don't get a big head, nigga," Tirzah said. "You a'ight, but you ain't all that."

"Hater alert." Rell laughed. As he left out the door, he looked back and saw Tamera give Tirzah a light punch in the arm.

King Rio

Chapter 5

Tamera fell back against the door and sighed while Tirzah rubbed away the pain in her arm.

"Hit me again, bitch," Tirzah warned, pouting.

"You're trying to run off the finest nigga I done seen," Tamera said. "You know all the bullshit Kendrick put me through. I need a good nigga. Especially a fine one. That nigga Rell is fine as fuck. And his daddy owns the fucking building. You need to be trying to see what his brother looks like."

Tirzah's pout turned into a smirk. "If he looks anything like him, I'm on his ass."

Tamera took off to the living room window, and Tirzah was a second behind her. She raised the blinds, and they looked down at the snow-covered street below just as Rell came jogging down the porch stairs.

There was a white Impala parked right in front of Tamera's car, and idling next to the Impala was a red SUV. Tamera couldn't see much of the teenager that got out of the SUV's passenger door other than the fact that he was dark-skinned and had on a black leather Pelle Pelle coat over baggy jeans and black sneakers. She saw Rell take a large pile of cash out of a front pocket and flip through it until he found the bill he needed. He passed the bill in to the driver through the passenger window.

"Bitch, you see all that money?" Tirzah said in disbelief. "What the hell did he do, keep all the rent money?"

"I don't know. I'm not thinking about his money."

"You need to be. Kendrick ain't sending you nothing."

Tamera rolled her eyes and stared at Rell. He was walking up the stairs next to his brother, talking and glancing around. Lil Zo and a few other gang members who were standing on the corner had shifted their attention to Rell when he pulled out the bankroll. Rell didn't seem to notice, but Tamera and Tirzah did.

"Look at them thirsty-ass niggas," Tirzah said. "You see how they looked at that money?"

"Of course I saw it." Tamera lowered the blinds as Rell and his brother entered the building. She went and sat down on the arm of the sofa. "He must not know how thirsty these niggas around here can be."

"Must not," Tirzah agreed.

"Damn, that nigga is so fine, girl. Mmm."

"If he come down here with his brother, I'm fuckin' that li'l nigga." Tirzah said it without a lick of shame in her voice. "You better do the same to Rell. That's the kinda nigga you can't just let slip by without at least trying to keep him. He got a car and his daddy owns the building we live in. And I think I remember Big Man saying something about some other houses he owns around here somewhere."

"If I do fuck the nigga, it ain't gonna be because his daddy owns the building. I'm not a gold-digger."

"But you ain't fuckin' with no broke niggas." Tirzah laughed aloud. She walked to the kitchen, mumbling something about having left the blunt burning. When she came back, she turned on the TV and pressed play on the bootleg copy of *Straight Outta Compton* they'd gotten a few months ago.

"I'm tired of this damn movie," Tamera complained. "I wanna get fucked up today. You wanna go to the L?" The L was code for the liquor store.

Tirzah nodded her head yes to the idea. "Hell yeah. We get Rell and his brother drunk, you know what's going down."

A glorious smile crossed Tamera's face as she envisioned herself in bed with Rell. She inhaled sharply and then exhaled.

She was high as ever off the Kush and grimly determined to make something out of this cold December day.

She dug in her purse and fished out two twenty-dollar bills. "We can get a fifth."

"Henny?" Tirzah asked.

"And you know it!" Tamera said excitedly.

She and Tirzah put on several layers of clothes in preparation for the ice-cold weather before heading out: matching black sweatpants and hoodies over thermals, gloves, and skullcaps. As they were getting in the car, Lil Zo, one of the boys on the corner, shouted a question to them.

"Ay, y'all know them niggas who just went in the building a few minutes ago?"

Chapter 6

"Watch out for them niggas standing out there on that corner," Jah said as he kicked off his shoes and fell back across
the sofa. "Look like they was on one."

Rell was in the refrigerator, getting another beer. He replied to his brother's warning by taking the pistol out of his
back pocket and yanking back the slide to chamber a round as
he walked into the living room.

There was a small knot on Jah's forehead. The back of
his right hand was all scraped up. His bottom lip was split on
the side. His brand-new coat was ripped across the back.

As bad as Rell wanted to fuck somebody up over his little
brother being hurt, he knew he had to keep a cool head about
it. If he went and found the man who'd fought Jah, he knew
he'd be risking another prison bid, and that was something he
wanted to avoid. Plus, he knew that even if he got away with
killing the guy, it would only bring more drama.

Jah pulled a handgun out of his jacket. It had an extended
clip protruding from its bottom. He laid it on his chest and
stared up at the ceiling. He had the dark complexion of their
father, and he was as thin as a rail, but other than that, he was
Rell's twin. They shared the same handsome facial structures
and slender noses, the same prudent brown eyes, and they
even walked alike.

"They killed D-Lo, bruh," Jah said, his tone heavy with
emotion. "I still can't believe it."

"Who did it?"

"One of the C's."

The C's Jah was referring to were Conservative Vice
Lords. Although Rell and Jah were both members of practi-
cally the same gang, they were from a different "branch" of
the Vice Lords. They were Travelers, which was the gang that

ran their block on 13th and Avers as well as the neighborhood that they were in right now. Rell didn't know the guys on the corner, but he was certain that they, too, were Travelers. Not like he cared what gang they were in. He didn't know them and they didn't know him, which meant that neither of them would hesitate to make him a victim if and when they ever got the chance.

"I think his name Stain," Jah went on. "Some shit like that. I fought the nigga head up. Nigga hit like a bitch. All he could do was grab me, slam me. Hoe-ass nigga tore my coat."

"You say y'all came back shootin'? What happened? Y'all missed?" Rell was concerned about the shooting, especially since his brother was involved.

Jah shook his head from side to side. His eyes wouldn't leave the ceiling. "I hit one of the niggas. Just didn't get him where it counted. They say he caught one in the arm. Another li'l nigga caught two to the leg. And D-Lo…he got hit when they shot back at us. Shit, it was so dark. And we came from out the cut, from the gangway. I thought we had 'em."

"Well, you thought wrong."

"I'm gon' catch his ass," Jah promised.

"You gon' leave that shit alone for right now. That's what the fuck you gon' do." Rell took a seat in the black leather easy chair that Big Man usually sat in. Cracking open the Budweiser, he turned to the Bears game just as they were kicking off against the Arizona Cardinals.

A couple of minutes into the game, Jah sat up and rolled a blunt for himself.

Rell was trying his best to focus on the game, but Tamera's pretty face was on his mind. He realized that he'd failed to get an answer from her letting him know if she was single or not.

"Li'l bruh," he said suddenly, "you gotta see the girls who live right up under Pops. Tamera and Tirzah, bruh. Bad. On Neal."

Jah looked at Rell, intrigued. "Yeah?"

"Man, super bad. Both of 'em thick, and they not ugly at all. I'm talkin' pretty as fuck, bruh. I'm on Tamera, but you might be able to get her snitchin'-ass sister."

"Aw, hell nah. She a snitch? What the fuck I'ma do with her?"

"Not like that. I just call her that 'cause she told Tamera what I said when I first walked in."

"Sounds like we need to be down there!" Jah spoke with a sudden burst of energy. "Shit, I gotta make sure they don't know my BM first. I'm not about to go through that again. You remember what happened last time we got on some hoes together."

Of course Rell remembered. Felicia Saunders, the mother of Jah's newborn daughter, was seven months pregnant when she was tipped off that Jah and Rell were together in a house full of women. They were just getting ready to fuck two of the girls on the living room sofa when Felicia and her sister Candace walked in the door (it hadn't been locked) and beat up every girl in the house before Jah and Rell were able to drag them back outside. Felicia ended up catching a felony assault charge for the incident, and she had only recently begun to allow Jah to come around her again.

"Yeah," Rell said with a brief chuckle, "you're right. Maybe you need to stay up here. We wouldn't want that."

"Yeah, right. Fuck Felicia. That bitch been leaving Dora with Momma almost every day of the week, all so she can go out with her ugly-ass friends. I'm doin' me. As long as they don't know her, it's cool. Shit, nigga, fuck this game. Let's slide on them now. We can bring 'em up here. Pops ain't gon' be back for how long? Two weeks? Nigga, we can have a ball. We need some drinks, some more loud. It's crackin'."

Rell shook his head no. "We gotta show some respect. Pops specifically told me not to bring nobody up in here. I gotta honor that. Now, what we can do is go down there and chill with them."

Jah put on a conspiratorial smirk. "Netflix and chill." He nodded his head. "Yeah, I'm with that." He laughed. "Man, where you get that big-ass bankroll from? Pops gave you all that?"

Rell nodded.

"Man, that's some bullshit. He didn't tell you to give me none?"

"Nope." Rell happily turned up his beer and took two refreshing gulps. He had cotton mouth from smoking so much weed today. Though he intended to give Jah a few hundred dollars out of the money, he wasn't going to tell Jah just yet. For one, he wanted to take Jah shopping with the money instead of just giving it to him, knowing that Jah would undoubtedly spend it all on drugs and liquor with his friends if he got ahold of it.

There was one thing Rell had to admit, though: the liquor idea with Tamera and Tirzah sounded like fun.

A few minutes later when he got up to use the bathroom, Rell took $250 out of the big wad of cash and then went looking around in his father's bedroom for a place to stash the rest of it. His main reason for choosing the bedroom was because it was locked. Big Man had left him a set of keys to the door's two deadbolt locks.

"In case of an emergency," Big Man had said. "Got my shotgun on the shelf in the closet, already loaded and all. Just point it at the fucker and let him have it." Big Man had said it as if he was expecting some specific intruder to come by when he left.

Rell had laughed then, and now as he rummaged around through the many jewelry boxes on one of the two wooden nightstands, he found himself laughing again.

Pops was right to be concerned.

There were expensive-looking pieces of jewelry in the boxes. Gold and diamond necklaces, earrings, and rings.

One ring caught Rell's attention. It was Susan's engagement ring, and it wasn't in either of the jewelry boxes. It was just laying on the dresser, next to a comb and a folded silk Gucci headscarf.

Rell picked the ring up and studied its huge white diamond. Big Man was known for bragging about how much he'd paid for the ring.

"My first hundred grand went to this damn thing," he'd often say, and Rell believed him.

The ring had one large, flawless 9-carat round cut white diamond surrounded by a bunch of smaller white diamonds.

Just then, Rell's smartphone rang, and his heart stopped when he saw Big Man's mobile number pop up. Instinctively, he looked around the room in search of a camera, thinking that Pops had to have seen him going through their things.

He answered the call. "Yeah, what's up, Pops?"

"Susan done left her ring on the dresser. Can you go in my bedroom and see if it's in there? Make sure she ain't lost the damned thing. Should be on the dresser. That's where she claims she left it."

Rell heard Susan in the background. "I ain't claimed shit, David. I know where I left my ring. It's right on top of my scarf."

Big Man said, "She say it's on her scarf. Take a look for me before we end up missing this flight."

Rell told Pops to hold on and went to the door to make a bit of noise, making it sound like he was just now unlocking it. He scrunched his nose at the overpowering odor that seemed to be embedded in the bedroom's walls. It smelled just like Susan's perfume and Big Man's funk.

Finally, he went back to the dresser and said, "Yeah, it's right here, Pops. What you want me to do with it?"

Big Man said something to Susan, then, "Just, uh...when we get to Florida, just mail it to me. Express mail. Overnight. Can you do that?"

"Yeah, I'll do it. Soon as you gimme the address. Just call and let me know where to send it."

"Okay. Don't lose that damn ring, son. Put it up right now, and don't touch it until I tell you otherwise."

"I got'chu, Pops."

Rell ended the call and put the ring in a white porcelain jewelry box on Susan's nightstand.

He decided to keep the big pile of cash in his jeans pocket after all. He was strapped, Jah was strapped — there was nothing to worry about.

Leaving out of the bedroom, he didn't lock the door. He knew he'd be right back in there to get the ring when Pops called for it in a couple of hours, and until then, he planned on being seated in Big Man's comfy old easy chair, drinking Big Man's Budweiser and watching the Chicago Bears game on Big Man's television.

Chapter 7

It was just eighteen degrees outside.

Tirzah was too cold to get out of the car, so she stayed put and kept the windows shut to trap the heat inside with her while Tamera went in Anna's Food and Liquors on 13th and Kedzie Avenue.

Tamera had left the radio blasting. A Beyoncé song came on, and Tirzah began bobbing her head to it. She thought about Rell and his brother and hoped she'd be able to get some dick today. She most certainly wasn't going to call on Lil Webb - not after all the drama she'd gone through fucking with him yesterday.

She took her smartphone out of her purse and logged into Facebook to see what was going on in the city. It didn't surprise her to see that D-Lo, one of the younger guys she knew from off Avers, had been killed in yet another gang-related shooting. Everyone was posting their RIP's, saying how much of a good guy D-Lo was and that he didn't deserve to die at such a young age. A girl claiming to be pregnant with his baby had changed her profile picture to a photo of him with angel wings on his back. A few of D-Lo's friends were promising retaliation against the "opps" who'd taken his life.

"Shit is about to start going down again," Tirzah said, shaking her head as she continued to scroll down her page.

When she saw that there was nothing else to be seen, she went to the search bar and typed in 'Sharon LadySavage Welch'. It was the page that belonged to Lil Webb's side chick, the girl Tirzah had fought last night.

Tirzah figured that by now she'd be blocked, but that wasn't the case at all. She and Sharon were still friends — well, Facebook friends.

It was clear by Sharon's last three posts that the two of them were anything but friends.

'Soooo why did I end up having to whoop my punk ass baby daddys gf last night cuz the thot bitch don't know her place'

'All the hoe did was buss my lip n gimme a few scratches. I pumpkin headed that hoe'

'I'm still friendz with the bitch, I ain't blockin that hoe she gon see me umma make ha block me or she gon b blockin deez nucklez again ol big face ass bitch'

Tirzah could only snicker and shake her head in disbelief. She looked at the comments (there were more than fifty on each post, along with all kinds of emojis) and gritted her teeth. Some of the instigators were girls who called themselves friends of Tirzah's, which pissed her off even more.

She went to the first post and was just about to post a snide comment when someone knocked on her window. She turned to look and was surprised to see that it was Sharon's dad. He was almost as big as Big Man, and by the swelling over his left eye, it looked like he'd taken an ass-whooping just like his daughter.

"Ain't you the bitch my daughter got into it with?" he asked, stooped down and snarling at her. He had on a thick blue jacket and a matching Colts skullcap. His face was uglier than Tirzah ever remembered it being - bumpy and dry and crusty. His lips were chapped.

"Nigga, if you don't get the fuck away from me." Tirzah rolled her eyes and turned her attention back to her smartphone, though out of the corner of her eye she kept watching him.

"Put cha hands on my baby again and I'ma put mine on you," he threatened, slapping a hand on the roof. "I don't know what the hell's wrong with you young muthafuckas, but you niggas got me fucked up. I just had to beat the shit out a nigga last night. Don't think I won't put my hands on you the same fuckin' way."

As bad as Tirzah wanted to cuss the man out, she kept her cool, and he walked off into Anna's just as Tamera came walking out carrying three plastic bags.

When Tamera got in, she immediately noticed that Tirzah was upset.

"Just drive," Tirzah said. "And the next time we leave out the house, make sure you remind me to bring the baseball bat with us."

King Rio

Chapter 8

The Kush must have been stronger than Jah could handle, because it had him snoring by halftime.

Rell took the gun off Jah's lap and put it on the coffee table. He was on his fifth beer and feeling a decent buzz, and he was so high that he'd eaten an entire big bowl of leftover spaghetti during the halftime show, but that wasn't stopping him from rolling another blunt in his last cigarillo.

His smartphone rang just as he was lighting the blunt. It was Erica calling.

She went right in on him. "Nigga, I know yo' momma told you I came by the house earlier. Where you at?"

"Watchin' the game at my pops' crib. Why? The hell you want?"

"You hear about D-Lo?"

"Yeah, I heard."

"You better watch out for yo' li'l brother. Keep his li'l bad ass with you. My girl Trina just told me she heard some niggas was s'posed to be at his head about the shit that went down with D-Lo last night."

"Yeah? Where she hear that at?"

"From some niggas on 16th and Millard. Her grandma stay right up the street from Dvorak. That's where I just came from. On my way to Trumbull to get some weed now, then I'm out south with my li'l sister."

"A'ight. I'll catch up with you."

"Be safe, nigga."

"I'm good."

"Can I come and see you before I head out south? You know I need my fix."

"Every nigga out here got a dick you can jump on," Rell said.

He grinned at the sound of Erica sucking her teeth indignantly.

"You are definitely right about that," she retorted, her tone replete with attitude.

"Yup." Rell hit end on her and put his phone back on the charger. He and Erica went through this all the time, and she never had a problem jumping on a random dick when he wasn't acting right. Today he didn't care as much as he sometimes did.

Tamera was to thank for him not giving a fuck. He wanted her so badly that there was no way he'd risk upsetting her by bringing another girl over. If anything, he'd bring her instead of Erica up to his father's apartment.

The idea of him fucking Tamera made his dick harden in his jeans, so much so that he had to adjust himself to make it more comfortable.

"Damn," he mumbled aloud to himself, "Tamera needs to bring her ass up here. I'll break the rules for her sexy ass. Fuck what Pops got to say about it."

A sudden thump and a scratching noise outside the front door startled him. He got up, pushing down the bulge in his jeans, and took the gun off his hip as he went to the door.

"Yo," he said, putting an eye to the peephole just as he heard yet more scratching at the door.

The noise ceased.

He could see nothing in the hallway.

"The fuck goin' on out here?" Rell muttered as he unlocked and then opened the door.

The dark gray cat looked up at Rell and hissed at him before zipping around his boot and into the apartment. Rell laughed. He'd almost forgotten about the cat. It was big and extra furry, with a mean scowl permanently molded on its face and a matching attitude.

Rell put the gun in his back pocket and was getting ready to close the door when he heard the voice he'd been wanting to hear.

Tamera and Tirzah were downstairs talking. It sounded like they were coming up the stairs to their apartment.

He had to say something, so he said, "Y'all quiet down with that shit. My daddy ain't here, nigga. This a new sheriff in town."

The two sisters went silent for half a second. Then Tamera shouted up to him.

"Come down here and shut me up. Fuck you mean," Tamera replied jokingly.

A smile grew on Rell's face as the girls appeared at the bottom of the staircase on the fourth floor. They looked up at him with the same expression Life the cat had worn a moment prior.

He busted out laughing.

"We beat up landlords, too," Tirzah warned.

"For real, for real," Tamera added.

Rell gave them two thumbs down. "I don't beat on women, but I will definitely defend myself." He turned to step back into the apartment, and against his father's orders he said, "Y'all can come in if y'all want to. We ain't doing shit but watching the game. Well, I am. Li'l bruh done passed out on me."

He saw them glance at each other, then Tamera started up the stairs, followed reluctantly by Tirzah. He stepped aside as they walked in, and was tempted to touch Tamera's perfectly round derrière as she passed by him. The wonderful scent of her perfume was overwhelming. She gave him the side eye and a sexy little smirk.

Tirzah gave him an irritated expression and a suck of the teeth.

"Fuck out my face." Rell raised a hand, as if he were getting ready to backhand Tirzah into the middle of next week.

She ducked quickly and yelped as she ran up behind Tamera.

"Scary ass," Rell said, grinning widely as he shut and locked the door.

There was only the one sofa and the easy chair, and since Jah was stretched out on the sofa sleeping, Tirzah sat on the arm of it that was closest to the easy chair.

Which is how Rell got lucky.

He sat down in the easy chair, and without saying a word Tamera sat on his right knee and leaned forward to put her bags on the table.

"This the kinda shit I like right here," he said, cheesing and putting his hands on her hips.

"Shut up." Tamera slapped his other knee. "Let me tell you what just happened to my sister while I was in the store."

"I'll tell him," Tirzah said. "This dirty-ass old man banged on my window and threatened me 'cause I beat his daughter's ass last night. It's crazy because I was just about to comment on some slick shit the bitch posted on Facebook when the nigga popped up at my window. Ol' musty-lookin' nigga from off Millard. He lucky I didn't have my bat. I sure would've went upside his goddamn head with it. It's all good, though. I just messaged that hoe on FB and told her it's on and crackin' next time I see her mu'fuckin' ass, since she wanna run and tell her daddy on me."

"We need to get us a gun, Tirzah. I told you that two weeks ago." Tamera cracked open a bottle of Hennessy and asked Rell if there was any ice.

Rell nodded his head yes. He saw that Tirzah had her eyes on Jah's gun on the coffee table as she got up and went to the kitchen with three red plastic cups for the ice.

Tamera was also studying the gun.

"Jesus Christ," she said. "Look at that clip. Why's it so—how many bullets does it hold?"

Rell shrugged, though he knew that it was a 9 millimeter Ruger pistol with a 32-shot clip and one in the chamber. "That's just too much," Tamera said. "A handgun with a machine gun clip. I understand, though. With the way these young niggas around here been shootin', you need something like that."

Rell rubbed his hands on her hips. The softness of them brought back his erection. He stopped rubbing and checked his smartphone for no reason other than to get rid of the hard-on before Tamera saw it and started thinking of him as some sort of pervert.

He had two new text messages from Momma:

'Don't forget to drop me off some money. I need at least 100'

'Is Jah there? Tell him Felicia just brought his baby over and I'm not about to babysit all day either'

Rell leaned forward and put the smartphone down on the coffee table. He was much too preoccupied with Tamera to reply to a text from anyone. He knew his mom was probably drinking and high off the Xanax pills she took just about every day. She'd be alright. He'd stop by later and drop off at least $150. She'd be more than happy with that.

Jah rolled over on the sofa just as Tirzah came back with the ice-filled cups. Tirzah and Tamera gasped in unison.

"I know him," Tirzah said. "That's Jah. Felicia's baby-daddy."

"He's your brother?" Tamera asked Rell.

He nodded. "Yeah."

"I've been over his house before. Oh, so you're the brother who was in prison? I heard about you."

Just then, Jah sat up and immediately looked at the two sisters. He yawned, his expression grumpy and groggy. He snatched his gun off the table and put it on his lap. Tirzah plopped down next to him.

"Yeah?" Rell said to Tamera. "What did you hear about me?"

"I heard you was with the shits before you went down. They say you fucked up ol' boy, broke his whole face or something like that. Pistol-whipped him."

"They say a lot o' shit."

Jah said, "I know them. They came to the crib wit' Felicia one day when you was in the joint."

"Yeah," Tamera said, "I used to work with her at Woodfield Mall. I drove her home every day when she didn't have a car. That's back when I had my white Intrepid. She was young then, like sixteen or seventeen, I believe."

Jah got up, mumbled something about him having to take a piss, and went off to the bathroom with his gun in hand. Tamera stood to pour the drinks. She had a couple of bottles of Pepsi but Rell took his drink straight. Tirzah took a pack of Backwoods cigarillos out of one bag, and Rell tossed her the rest of his sack of Kush to roll.

Taking a big gulp of the cognac, Rell's face twisted. He hissed and gagged.

"See." Tamera laughed. "Should've cut that shit with some of this Pepsi. Tough ass."

"I'm good." Rell took another sip to prove his point. "I'm a big dog, li'l mama. Grown-ass man."

"Oh, shut up."

"I'm for real. I'll drink the whole bottle and still be good."

"You drink that bottle, you gon' pay for it. Bet you that much."

"I ain't payin' for shit." Rell put a hand on Tamera's thigh and gave it a squeeze.

"I don't know why you keep feeling all on me, boy. Calm down. I don't even know you like that yet."

"Yet." Rell nodded. "Keyword. Yet. You gon' get to know me real good."

Tamera smiled and rolled her eyes.

For the next couple of minutes, they sat and drank while Tirzah told Rell about the fight she'd had with some girl named Sharon last night. When Jah returned, he wasted no time getting a cup of ice for himself and pouring up. Rell didn't mind letting his little brother drink at seventeen. All the teenagers were doing it, and he preferred to have Jah drink with him rather than with the guys in the streets.

Tirzah got a phone call from hers and Tamera's mother, and Rell took the opportunity to get in a one-on-one conversation with Tamera.

"So," he asked, "you never told me if you're single or not. I'm guessing you are single since you're sitting all on my dick right now."

"Since when did a knee become a dick?"

Rell laughed. "You think that's my knee."

"Boy, you need to stop."

"Okay, I see you don't wanna tell me."

Tamera sighed. "I'm single," she said finally. "I had a boyfriend, but his trifling ass had two kids by some other bitches while we were together. Now he's in Stateville. He thinks I'm still his, but I haven't been going to see him or nothing like that. He used to live with me, had an apartment downstairs that he was trapping out of. It got raided. They gave him twenty years since it was his fourth arrest for dealing, but he filed an appeal. Lawyers say he might get the charges dropped. I don't know."

Rell nodded. He remembered Big Man telling him about the raid that had gone down a while back. He'd been on house arrest at the time.

"What about you?" Tamera asked. "Who you been fuckin'? I know a fine-ass nigga like you got a girl."

"Nah, not really."

"What's that supposed to mean?"

"Just what I said. I got Erica, and we fuck every now and then, but that's about it. I ain't got no real girlfriend. Shit, I just got off house arrest not too long ago. Ain't really had time to find one."

"Well, if you fuck with me, I'm not going for anybody else. I don't do the sharing."

Rell didn't mind being faithful to a woman as beautiful as Tamera. He didn't mind at all.

The Henny heightened his buzz instantly. Suddenly he was hot, and it wasn't because the heat was on 90. He took off his sweatshirt and draped it over the back of the chair.

Tamera's eyes went to his arms, and he was glad that he'd tightened up his body during his prison bid. His arms were huge. Tamera rubbed them, the corner of her bottom lip tucked behind her upper teeth. He figured since she was rubbing, he would rub, too. His hands went to her waist, and then to her thighs. Again her perfume drifted into his nostrils. Her ass felt so soft on him. He almost pulled her into his lap so that she could feel what she was doing to him, but he kept his composure.

"Will you two niggas get a room or somethin'?" Tirzah said, hating.

Everyone laughed. The liquor was flowing, and they were becoming comfortable with each other. Rell glanced at the score on the game a few times, but he was much more into Tamera.

Tirzah and Jah started talking.

Rell leaned forward, put his mouth right behind Tamera's left ear.

"Let's go in the back right quick," he suggested in a whisper. His mind was on the guest bedroom that he and Jah usually slept in whenever they stayed the night at Big Man's.

Tamera didn't reply with words. She shook her head no, smirking happily. She finished off her drink and then stood up, pulling him up with her by his wrist.

"Nasty-ass hoe," Tirzah said, laughing as Rell and Tamera headed out of the living room.

Chapter 9

Tamera's heart was pounding against her ribcage. The cognac and the feel of Rell's erection pressing against her ass had her nipples hard and her pussy soaking wet.

He led her into a bedroom that was empty except for a queen-sized bed with two fuchsia-colored sheets on it and an open closet that was filled almost to the ceiling with women's shoeboxes.

"I've always wanted to come up here and see how Big Man's place looked," Tamera said as she sat down on the foot of the bed. "I thought it'd be more...lavish. Well, don't get me wrong, the living room looks nice, but there ain't nothing in here. This room looks abandoned."

"It is." Rell shut the door. "They sleep together. This room is really just for me and Jah."

"I think I remember seeing D-Lo with Jah when I dropped Felicia off one day. Was that one of his friends?"

Rell nodded.

"Damn." Tamera shook her head. "These young niggas out here nowadays don't even care about taking a life. Ain't no more fighting. Whatever happened to fistfights? What happened to black love? Is that shit becoming extinct?"

"Nope." Rell stepped in front of her and put his hands on her thighs. "I got some black love for you."

"I just bet you do." She looked up at him, wondering if she should ask him to wear a condom or if she should just let it happen. As fine as Rell was, she knew she wouldn't mind an accidental pregnancy by him. At least her baby would be cute.

Why am I thinking about a baby? she thought, and then let out a giggle.

"The fuck you laughin' at?" Rell asked.

"Nothing. I just...thought of something funny. It's nothing."

"Don't start with that crazy shit."

"Shut the fuck up, boy."

"Make me."

"Don't think I won't. You better ask my sister. Or better yet, ask your brother's girl. Felicia done seen me shut shit down on numerous occasions."

Rell wasn't trying to hear her war stories. He grabbed her by the waist and pushed her back on the bed. His strong brown hands unzipped her hoodie and lifted the shirt she wore underneath it. He freed her breasts from her bra and took a nipple in his mouth.

Tamera inhaled through her nose. His cologne drove her wild. He put a hand between her thighs and stroked the crotch of her sweatpants until she grabbed his hand and pushed it inside her panties.

"You got a condom?" she asked breathlessly.

Nodding his head yes, he went on sucking her breast, rubbing the other, slipping a probing finger into her slippery love tunnel.

She gasped. Her fingers massaged his scalp. She wanted to feel his dick in her hands, to see what he was working with, but she was content with the pleasure he was giving her now.

A part of her felt a little slutty for giving it up so quickly, but the liquor made her say fuck it. It wasn't like she did this every day. She hadn't fucked anyone since Kendrick. She deserved some good loving.

Seconds later, Rell rose up and unbuckled his Louis Vuitton belt.

Tamera gawked at his lower region until he had his fly open and he was whipping out his rigid love muscle. Her eyes went wide at the sight of it. He had the thickest dick she'd ever seen, and it was long, too. Maybe ten inches or so. Veiny. Bulbous-headed. Everything she wanted in a penis.

She snickered nervously. "Damn."

"Damn?" he said.

"It's a good damn," she said quickly. "A damn, damn, damn kinda damn. Mmm."

She sat up and put her hands on it. She squeezed, and a droplet of precum oozed out.

Although she had rarely given Kendrick head, she felt compelled to put this particular dick in her mouth, and so she did.

First she sucked on the head, stroking the rest of his length in her hands. She couldn't believe how huge it was, and how good it tasted.

Rell put a hand on the back of her head, and she went to work, sucking as much as she could into her mouth every time her head went forward. She rubbed and pulled down on his balls with one hand and stroked his fat sausage with the other as she tightly sucked him. He thrust his hips forward, and she choked as the head hit the back of her throat, but she didn't stop or slow down. She wanted to reel Rell all the way in and keep him under her spell, and she knew exactly how to do it.

He took a Magnum condom out of his pocket and bit it open, but Tamera wasn't quite ready for him to put it on. She kept sucking him until he yanked his dick from between her lips and stumbled back to the white stucco wall behind him.

Tamera wiped her mouth and laughed.

"Damn, Superhead," Rell said, breathing hard.

Turning over on all fours, Tamera took off her sweatpants and the boy shorts she wore under them. She arched her back and wiggled her hips, looking over her shoulder at him, expecting him to put on the condom and dig right in.

Rell had other plans.

He kneeled down, turned his back to her, and hit her with a Matrix-like move, leaning backward so that his mouth was right under her pussy.

She shuddered when his tongue touched her clitoris. His fingertips dug into the flesh of her ass as he began licking her. He slapped her ample bottom several times. The rough slaps turned Tamera on. She dropped down on his face and let out a moan, biting the center of her lower lip.

Rell went on tonguing her for over ten minutes, which is when she began to tremble and wind her hips in orgasm. He kept licking for a few more seconds before standing up and putting the condom on.

He rubbed the back of his neck. "That was a fucked up position," he said. "Damn near broke my mu'fuckin' neck. Horny-ass girl."

"Sorryyyy." Tamera giggled, dragging out the word.

The sight of his monster pole made her pussy quiver. She watched him roll the rubber onto it and step forward, grabbing ahold of her waist.

She wanted to tell him to take it easy on her. She hadn't gotten busy in a long while, and his dick was bigger than she'd expected.

But then he pushed the head in, and then a few more inches, and she put her face in a pillow as her pussy was stretched wider than it had ever been before. Face twisted, she released open-mouthed moans into the pillow and took it like a woman.

Rell showed little sympathy. Once he established a rhythm, he held her hips in a firm grip and punished her. He slapped her ass a couple of times and slid the palms of his hands all across the jiggling cheeks. She could tell that he was enjoying himself without even looking back at him. He spoke a few one-word sentences.

"Damn. Shit. Yeah..."

Kendrick was the furthest thing from Tamera's mind. She couldn't believe she was giving it up to Rell on the first day. She'd never done it before. Of the three other men she'd had sex with in the past, she'd made them all wait at least a week or two. Even when one of them — Twan, a Gangster Disciple from Englewood — offered to eat her pussy after their first date, she'd turned him down.

So why was she face down with her ass up in the air, getting her brains fucked out by this ridiculously handsome stranger?

She chalked it up to him being ridiculously handsome. Rell was one of the finest niggas she'd ever seen, tall and light-skinned with the most perfect face and chiseled body. He looked like he could be a personal trainer, or maybe a popular male model.

He turned her over on her back and gave her a hard kiss on the lips as he shoved his dick in and went ham, pushing one of her legs up so that her foot was almost touching the wooden headboard.

He took off his shirt. Tamera was able to read the tattoo that curved around the front of his neck like the collar of a shirt. It was the word SOLID over a big letter T, which she knew meant that he was a member of the TVL's. She wasn't surprised. In Chicago's ghettos, just about everybody was affiliated with one gang or another, and here in "Holy City", where the Vice Lords were founded, most of the guys were members of a branch of VL's.

Tamera didn't mind, as long as Rell wasn't a gangbanger. There were gang members and then there were gangbangers. The bangers rarely survived long on the streets without getting killed or sentenced to life in prison for killing someone else.

The thought of Rell's gang affiliation was a fleeting one. His rapid thrusts had Tamera's mind all over the place. She put her hands on his lower back and pulled him in deeper.

Chapter 10

Jah was glad that Tirzah hadn't judged him for having a girl-friend.

Just minutes after they first heard Rell and Tamera going at it in the bedroom, Tirzah put a hand in his lap and massaged his dick through his jeans until he leaned back and pulled it out.

Now she was slurping it in and out of her throat. She had a hand under his shirt, exploring his chest as her head bobbed.

This was a good thing for Jah. The bomb head was keeping his mind off D-Lo's murder. As bad as he wanted to go over to 16th and Millard and shoot the first person he saw out there, he was content with sitting here on his father's couch with his dick in this dime piece's mouth. He'd wanted to fuck her when he first saw her with her sister and Felicia. Like Felicia, Tirzah was a bad bitch, a pretty redbone with a fat ass and neighborhood popularity. He could remember one day seeing her and her sister drive by on Avers and hearing all his guys talk about how bad the two girls were. He wondered if his guys would believe him if he told them that Tirzah sucked him off on his father's sofa.

He was already feeling a little drunk off the cognac, and the Kush had him feeling a little drowsy. He had a hand on Tirzah's ass, squeezing it as she deep-throated him. He dropped his head back and shut his eyes.

The room spun out of control.

"Damn, I'm halfway fucked up already," he muttered, his hand moving to her lower back and then up to the nape of her neck.

The sucking sounds of Tirzah's mouth was music to his ears. He wanted to fuck her, but he didn't have any condoms and he wasn't trying to end up with another baby. Felicia was a big enough headache.

Which is why he didn't stop Tirzah or even warn her that he was about to cum. He just let it happen and smiled as she kept sucking until his dick stopped twitching and spurting. Then she sat up slowly, smiling wider than he was. She got up and went to the trashcan in the kitchen. He saw her spit out a long rope of cum.

"You could've spit that shit out in the toilet or somethin'," Jah said, giving her a disgusted look. He was only joking. Tirzah could tell. She flipped him a middle finger and then rinsed out her mouth with cold water before returning to her seat next to him.

"Don't tell Felicia," she said. "I went to school with her. Me and that crazy bitch will be fighting all up and down Douglas."

"I ain't gon' say shit."

"You better not," Tirzah said.

"I said I won't, nigga. Don't be embarrassed now. You should've thought about that before you sucked this mu'fucka."

Tirzah sucked her teeth and pushed his shoulder. "Shut up. Tell me what happened to D-Lo. Wasn't he one of your friends? They say he got shot in the head."

"I don't know," Jah lied. "Wasn't there."

"They say a couple niggas got shot. That's crazy. I went to school with his cousin. He's like the fourth or fifth young nigga to get killed out here in the past few months. Niggas act like they can't fight no more. Everybody gotta shoot. It's sad."

"Niggas ain't fightin' no more." Jah picked up his Ruger. "If you out here in these streets and ain't got a pole with at least a thirty in it, you might as well get some life insurance and tell your momma you love her, 'cause it's over when the niggas you get into it with catch up with you. For real. They playing for keeps out here."

Tirzah shook her head and sighed. She poured herself another shot of cognac and mixed it with Pepsi.

She was raising the cup to her mouth when they heard the first shout.

Chapter 11

Sharon swung open the minivan's sliding door and hopped out before it even stopped at the curb.

Utterly unattractive and about ninety pounds overweight, she was the naturally angry type, the kind of girl who took out all of her problems on others.

Today her victim would be Tirzah, the bitch who'd fucked her man and punched her one too many times last night, the bitch who'd just left a comment on her Facebook page letting people know who'd really won the fight.

Sharon was shouting before her shoe even reached the snow-covered curb. "Tirzah, bring your tough ass outside! I'm out here, bitch, now what!"

The driver of the minivan was an equally obese dark-skinned girl named Nia. She lived in the same apartment building as Sharon. Derrick, Nia's brother, was in the passenger seat. They had come to record video of the fight to post on Facebook and to make sure that no one jumped in. Sharon wanted a rematch. Her lip was fat, and it didn't help that her father was also lumped up from a fight he'd been in last night.

There was a group of guys standing on the corner. Sharon knew them all. She knew everybody on Douglas Boulevard. She was the kind of girl that talked to everyone and learned all of their business to share it with everyone else.

But now she was the source of the gossip. People were talking about the fight she'd had with Tirzah. Those who'd seen it said she'd gotten her ass whooped. She had to make up for the loss.

It was cold outside, so unbearably cold that smoke poured out from her nose with every breath she took. The gloves she had on were doing little to keep her hands warm.

She screamed again. "Bitch, I know you hear me! All that Facebook talk ain't on shit, hoe! I'm out here! Come out here and talk that shit to my face!"

The guys on the corner started smiling and nodding. They obviously wanted to see some action, and Sharon was ready to give it to them.

She looked in through the glass door of the apartment building and saw Tirzah coming down the stairs in front of a dark-skinned teenager.

"Yeah, bitch," Sharon said, nodding and putting up her fists. "Round two, hoe. Let's get it."

Chapter 12

Tirzah knew right away that she was about to beat the brakes off Sharon's ass, and that's exactly what she did.

She rushed off the porch and immediately caught Sharon with a two-piece combo that knocked the fat girl into the piled up snow behind her. She quickly mounted Sharon and began pounding her face until it was covered in blood. Sharon couldn't fight a lick. The Hennessy was like fuel to the fiery hatred Tirzah had for the chubby girl, and she felt no need to guard herself against Sharon's friends. Not with Jah toting a gun with such a long clip on his hip.

She felt something breeze past the side of her head, as if someone had tried to hit her.

Then she heard Jah shout, "Bitch, you better get back 'fore you fuck around and get clapped."

Sharon gave up on trying to fight back and used her forearms to shield her bloodied face from Tirzah's blows. Droplets of blood splattered on the snow all around Sharon's head.

"This what you came for?" Tirzah was enraged. "This what the fuck you wanted? Huh? Huh, bitch? Come on, get up." She stood up and waited for Sharon to get up so that she could knock the fat bitch right back on her ass, but Sharon just curled up in a fetal position, holding her battered face and crying like a baby.

The next thing Tirzah knew Jah's arms were around her waist. He pulled her back onto the front porch of their building while she screamed at Sharon and watched as Sharon's two friends helped her up and pushed her into a minivan.

"Come back around here on that bullshit and I'ma pop yo' fat ass next time, hoe!" Tirzah shouted. "Fat-ass bitch! Fuck you and Webb."

"Calm down," Jah said in her ear. "Fuck that bitch. Let's just go back in the crib before the law pull down on us about this shit. As a matter of fact, we should leave just in case she call the police."

Tirzah struggled to regain her calm. The liquor had her on a hundred. She wanted to fight some more. Hell, the way she was feeling right now, she'd even fight Sharon's dirty-ass daddy.

The excited cheers from the dealers on the corner only made her adrenaline pump harder.

"Sis ain't gon' believe this shit," she said as she and Jah headed back into the building.

Following behind her, Jah chuckled and slapped her on the ass.

Tirzah didn't find anything funny.

"I can't believe that hoe came for me like that. Like I was some kinda fuckin' game to be played with. Bitches got me fucked up. I whoop bitches for breakfast."

Jah let out another laugh. "Not for breakfast."

"Shut up, Jah."

"That was funny as hell."

"No, what's funny is how that fat bitch had her hands up like she was about to get some hits off on me. That was hilarious."

"You didn't have to beat that girl up like that. It's obvious she can't fight."

"People who can't fight shouldn't come looking for a fight. That's why they made weapons."

"You say that shit now. If shorty come back strapped, I bet you have a change of heart."

"Whatever, Jah."

Tirzah wasn't trying to hear it. Sharon had gotten what she'd deserved. All that Facebook gangster talk had landed her in some shit she wasn't at all ready for.

King Rio

Chapter 13

By the time Rell ejaculated into the condom, both he and Tamera were all sweaty out of breath.

He pulled up his jeans and boxers, took off the used Magnum, tied it in a knot, and was just about to go to the bathroom to flush it when the door flew open.

What he saw shocked him.

Tirzah walked in looking pissed off with blood on her hands. Jah was right behind her.

"Sis, we need to be going somewhere right the fuck now. I just beat the shit out that bitch Sharon."

Tamera hopped up and dressed hurriedly while Jah filled them in on what had gone down.

The story was even more shocking. Rell couldn't believe he'd missed a whole fight. Well, then again, with the way he and Tamera had been going at it, he understood why they hadn't heard anything.

He put on his shirt and hoodie and buckled his belt.

"We gotta slide, bruh," Jah said.

"Nah." Rell shook his head no. "We're good up here. Even if they do call the law, we'll be good up here. If anything, I'll answer the door and say it's just me and you here. What you need to do is go down there and move her car. Pull it around the block. Park it in the alley on 15th and Homan. Tamera, give him the keys. I'll stay here with y'all."

They all went out to the kitchen. Suddenly the effects of the Hennessy were wearing off. Tamera gave Jah the keys to her car and then cussed out her sister for not coming to get her before the fight.

"I honestly didn't even know what was going on," Tirzah said, washing her hands in the sink. "I heard somebody yelling my name out, so I went to see what was up. Didn't realize it was her until I got downstairs and by then, I was ready to fight. I came straight out the door and beat her ass, right in front of her fat-ass friend. She brought that scary-ass bitch Nia and her brother with her. I should've whooped Nia's ass, too."

"Don't ever do that again, sis. Come get me first. Always come and get me first. I don't give a damn how you feel."

Jah put Tamera's keys on the table and shook his head. "That car gon' have to stay there," he said. "I got this pole on me. I'm not about to get pulled over tryna move a car around the block. Fuck that."

"Fine." Rell leaned back against the refrigerator and took a deep breath. The one thing he didn't want was the police barging into Big Man's building, not while he was supposed to be in charge. "Just...go lock the front door," he said finally.

"I did," Jah said, taking a seat at the table. He took out a pack of Newport cigarettes and lit one.

Tirzah turned her back to the sink and looked at Rell. Tamera stood beside Tirzah, shaking her head in disbelief.

Even now, looking frustrated and upset, with her hair in slight disarray and a simple pair of sweats on, Tamera was a beautiful sight to see. Rell couldn't keep his eyes off her.

After a moment of tense silence, the four of them filed back into the living room. Rell checked the front door to make sure that it was locked. He went to the easy chair and sat down. This time, Tamera chose to sit on the arm of the chair, while Tirzah and Jah returned to their seats on the sofa.

"They won't call the cops," Tirzah said. "Her family might come over here, though."

Jah put his cigarette in the ashtray, slumped over on the sofa, and groaned. "I'm slapped. Y'all on bullshit. I wouldn't have been drinkin' and smokin' like that if I knew this shit was gon' happen."

"You're too young to be drinking, anyway," Tamera said under her breath. She turned to Rell and pushed the tip of a forefinger in his right temple. "You shouldn't be letting him drink. He's not even old enough to drink."

"My li'l brother is grown," Rell said.

"Last time I checked, you had to be twenty-one to buy liquor. It's not normal for a seventeen-year-old to be drunk like that."

"It also ain't normal for a seventeen-year-old to see one of his best friends get killed right in front of him," Rell countered. "Shit, I would need a drink myself after seeing some shit like that."

"Who'd he get in a fight with?"

Rell shrugged. "Some older nigga on Millard. I wasn't there. Wish I would've been there. I'd have knocked out every nigga out there."

Tamera shook her head and sighed as she shifted her attention back to Tirzah, who was typing something on her smartphone.

Glancing at the television, Rell realized that the Bears game was over. His home team had lost.

"What are you doing?" Tamera asked Tirzah in the tone of voice people used when they suspected that someone was about to make a dumb mistake.

"I'm writing a post on Facebook telling that bitch—"

"Give me this"— Tamera snatched the smartphone from Tirzah and dropped it in Rell's lap —"fuckin' phone! Are you crazy? Look at all that blood you had on your hands. Do you really want to incriminate yourself on Facebook? Dummy. They build cases and prosecute people off Facebook posts. You do know that, right? Sit your drunk ass down and relax. Have another cup. Roll another blunt. Do something."

"We ain't got no more weed," Tirzah muttered vacantly.

Everyone looked at Rell, as if he was the answer to their marijuana prayers. He was also all out. He'd given up the last of his Kush for the last blunt they'd smoked.

"I can call Joseph," Tamera said, and all eyes moved to her. "He's the white guy I work with," she explained. "He gets his weed from Colorado, the legal Kush. It's the best shit I've smoked. He has, like, five different kinds of Kush, charges $50 for every quarter-ounce. He lives in Lincoln Park. Somebody will have to go and get it. His car's in the shop."

"I'm broke," Tirzah said quickly.

"Me too," Jah added.

"I got ten on it," Tamera said, going for her purse.

"You cheap-ass niggas." Rell took the large pile of cash out of the front left pocket of his jeans and peeled off two fifties. "Y'all ain't smokin' all my shit, either. Who gon' go and get it?"

"It'll have to be you or Jah," Tamera said.

Jah volunteered to go, but Rell was leery of his little brother's driving abilities after having watched him drink so much Hennessey. Jah's bloodshot eyes made it clear that he was under the influence.

He seemed to read Rell's mind. "Bruh, don't look at me like that. I ain't that slapped. You know we done got drunk and drove everywhere, nigga. I'm good. I can drive. Just gimme the money and the address."

"You dip in my sack, I'm fuckin' you up," Rell threatened as he handed the two fifty-dollar bills and the keys to his car to Jah.

Tamera sent a text message to Joseph asking for his address. He replied seconds later, and Jah typed it in his Google maps app before getting up, securing his gun on his hip, putting on his jacket, and heading for the door. To him, weed was worth the risk of riding dirty with the gun, as irrational as it may have been.

Eyeing the 32-round clip that poked out of Jah's torn jacket, Rell breathed in deeply and thought, *God, please watch over my crazy li'l brother and keep him from doing anything dumb in my car.*

Chapter 14

Tamera was beginning to like the look of Big Man's apartment.

When Jah left, she took his seat next to Tirzah and studied the many framed pictures on the walls, the coffee table, and end tables. There were pictures of Rell and Jah as kids, pictures of Big Man and Susan at their wedding. Over the television was a wood-framed painting of a black Jesus. On top of the China cabinet were more recent pictures of Rell and Jah.

A glass bowl full of pecans and walnuts sat in the middle of the glass-top coffee table, and beside it lay an iPad. The hardwood floor was spotless, except for the streaks of dirty wetness their shoes had tracked in.

"Can we watch a movie?" Tirzah asked. "I can't just sit here and watch ESPN. I'm not the sportsy type."

Rell tossed her the remote control and her smartphone. He was organizing his mound of cash into three piles on his lap.

There wasn't much cognac left in the bottle. Tamera poured the rest of it in her cup and waited for her sister to find something worth watching on TV, hoping that the fight with Sharon wouldn't lead to the police paying them a visit. She couldn't afford to bond Tirzah out of jail, and she knew their mother wouldn't lend any help. Momma hadn't sent them so much as a card since moving to Virginia.

She refocused on Rell. The memory of the hot sex they'd had gave her goosebumps.

Staring at him, she found it hard to believe that she'd been with someone so fine. She almost wanted to ask him to take off his shirt again, but she had to remind herself that Tirzah was in the room with them. She loved Tirzah, but she knew that Tirzah didn't discriminate when it came to sex.

They'd gotten into it twice in the past over Tirzah sleeping with one of her exes.

An elbow to the ribcage shook Tamera from her reverie. She turned to Tirzah and delivered an even harder elbow to Tirzah's arm. "Bitch. Don't elbow me. I ain't Sharon. I'll beat that ass," she said.

Tirzah giggled. "Stop staring at that boy like that," she whispered. "Thirsty ass."

A Grinch-like smile spread across Tamera's face. She leaned over to Tirzah. "Okay, I admit it," she whispered back, "the nigga got me sprung already. He's too fucking fine. Love at first sight."

"Y'all do know I'm sitting here, right?" Rell said.

Tamera and Tirzah laughed in unison, then Tirzah got all hyped up when she landed on VH-1 and saw Ray J. She'd had a crush on him for years.

Rell asked Tamera if she had any kids.

"No," she said. "What about you?"

He shook his head no. "I want some, though. One day. Not now, but definitely in the future. I want a daughter. If I have a son, I'm moving out of Chicago. It ain't a safe place to raise no boys."

"It really isn't."

"I don't even like having my li'l bruh out here."

"I bet you don't."

"Too dangerous," Rell said. "Niggas out here gettin' clapped up every day and night. I just got out the joint not too long ago. Ain't tryna go back, and I definitely ain't tryna go to the grave. I'm about to move in my own place and get in a college somewhere. Might just go and get my barber's license. I can already cut hair. Whatever I do, it won't be selling dope like I used to. Feds indicting niggas every other week."

Tamera gave a nod to Rell and then turned to the TV while he finished doing whatever he was doing to his money. She felt odd and uncomfortable for some reason. After a moment of contemplation, she chalked it up to it being the first time she'd slept with someone so quickly. Not that she regretted it. She knew that if she could go back in time she'd do it again.

The *Love and Hip Hop Hollywood* rerun wasn't good enough to hold her attention, and since Tirzah was already back on Facebook, she looked at Tirzah's phone to make sure there was no arguing going on.

Tirzah was only on Sharon's page for a few seconds before she was blocked. She chuckled once, logged out, and logged back in from Tamera's page. Just as Tirzah was typing Sharon's page name in the search bar, Rell got up from the chair.

"Come back in the room with me for a minute," Rell said.

Tamera didn't hesitate to hop up and follow him. She told Tirzah to stay on the fucking couch until they returned.

Feeling silly, she jumped on Rell's back when they made it into the hallway, locking her legs around his waist.

"If you don't get'cho fat ass off my back," he said, but he made no move to force her off as he walked in the bedroom, shut the door, and sat down on the bed.

She planted a kiss on the nape of his neck and hugged him tightly.

"I hope you know I don't just run around fucking every nigga I got a crush on," she said. "That was special."

"I hope it was." Rell rubbed her thighs and gave them a slap. "I just wanted to warn you about somethin'. It's about my li'l brother."

"What about him?"

"He's crazy."

"And? What's that supposed to mean?"

"Nothing really. I just hope your guy don't play no games. If it looks sweet, li'l bruh gon' pull it."

Tamera drew back, frowning at the back of Rell's head. She slipped from behind him and stood in front of him with her hands on her hips.

He fell back on his elbows and looked up at her, grinning widely, eyebrows raised.

"What do you mean, Rell? Joseph is one of my coworkers."

Rell shrugged. "Let's just hope nothing goes wrong," he said.

Chapter 15

2148 North Fremont Street was a quaint little white clapboard home with a small red car and a minivan of the same color parked out front.

Unlike Jah's neighborhood, the streets and sidewalks were completely cleared of snow. A white man in a white and blue blazer was walking by with his head down and his shoulders raised against the cold. His entire face was red. His hands were in his pockets, and he was moving fast.

"I thought white folks liked the cold," Jah said with a laugh as he turned off the engine and checked his rearview and sideview mirrors. "You mu'fuckas supposed to be out here in shorts and T-shirts."

He wondered if he should honk the horn or knock on the door. He didn't really want to go inside. Tamera had said that the guy was white, and Jah didn't trust white people. The only white people he was used to seeing wore badges and blue uniforms. He'd never been arrested, and he wanted to keep it that way.

"Fuck it," he said, and pushed open his door. He didn't want to alert the weed man's neighbors that he had company. They might already be on him about his dealings.

Jah put his head down and crossed the street to the address Tamera had given him. He looked both ways, halfway expecting to see a cop coming, then pressed the doorbell.

Five seconds later the door swung open, and Jah almost cracked up laughing.

"Hey, are you Tammy's friend? I'm Joseph. Come on in and close the door. Jesus, it's fucking freezing out there."

Joseph was skinnier than Jah, shirtless and wearing light blue jeans that had specks of paint all over the front. He had a red Mohawk and strange earrings that made large holes in his lobes. Tattoos of plain black skulls and bones covered the top of his back. The cuffs of his pants were torn and stringy. His sneakers were dirty and wide-looking.

Staring at Joseph, Jah stepped inside and kicked the door shut behind him. He walked into the filthiest living room he'd ever seen. On the dirty brown carpet were empty food containers, bent up and crushed soda cans, overturned cups, socks and shirts and underwear. A flat air mattress was in the middle of the floor. It looked like someone had spilled an entire bowl of noodles on it and never cleaned it up.

"Excuse the filth," Joseph said as he disappeared into a room up the hall. "My old lady's lazy as shit. Next time you stop by it'll look presentable. As soon as that whore gets off work this evening I'm making her clean this whole fucking place."

The stench was too much for Jah. He held his breath, his face scrunched tight. Then he put a forearm over his nose.

"Hurry up, man. This funky as shit. I don't know how the fuck you can live in this mu'fucka. Clean this shit up yourself."

"Can't, bro. Got things to do. Money to make. Weed to smoke." Joseph was all smiles as he came back to the living room holding two big bags of marijuana, one in each hand.

Jah's eyes went wide.

There had to be at least a pound in each bag. One of them looked orangeish. The other was bright green.

"Got Hawaiian Kush and Desert Dragon Kush," Joseph said, showing them to Jah. "The orange stuff's Hawaiian Kush. It'll sit you right flat on your ass, bro. Smoked a joint with my old lady the other night and all we did was sit and fucking stare at each other, bro. Shit's serious. The Desert Dragon's just as good, but it'll have you coughing like shit, and I think it lasts longer than the orange. Wanna test it out first? I'll roll one of each."

Slowly, a smile crept across Jah's face. He nodded once, unzipping his jacket. "I want all of it," he said, and drew the gun from inside his jacket.

He pointed the Ruger pistol at Joseph's face.

"Whoa, whoa...wait a minute. Hold on, bro." Joseph dropped the bags of Kush and raised his hands above his head. Fear grew in his eyes. "Ask Tamera, bro. I'm good people. I've never screwed anyone over. I'm...I'm good, bro."

"Shut the fuck up and lay down. Get on the floor. Don't make me pop yo' stupid ass. Get down or I'ma put you down." Jah's voice was as cold as the weather was outside.

Joseph hardly made it to one knee before Jah slammed the pistol across his forehead and sent him sprawling to the trash-littered carpet.

"Fuck! Come on, bro! You can have the shit! Just don't fucking hurt me!"

"Bitch, scream again. I dare you. I double dare you." Jah glanced around the room, searching for something to tie together Joseph's wrists. "Where the rest of it at? Where the money? And if you lie, I'm killin' yo' stupid ass."

"That's all of it, bro. I got about seven hundred bucks in my wallet. It's right there on the table. That's all I've got, bro. I swear on my mother's grave."

Jah found a raggedy belt next to the air mattress and used it to tie Joseph's hands behind his back. The scrawny guy groaned as Jah tightened the belt on his wrists.

"Bitch, if you make one mu'fuckin' move, I'ma blow your whole fuckin' head off," Jah threatened as he picked up the bags of Kush. He put them inside his jacket and zipped it closed. "I needed some bread for a new Pelle any mu'fuckin' way." He went to the wallet and took the cash from it.

Something told him that Joseph was probably lying about only having $700 in cash, but he wasn't tripping because the Kush was more than enough.

Pocketing the cash, he went back to Joseph and kicked the guy over onto his back.

"Please, man. Don't shoot me," Joseph pleaded. There was blood pouring out of a gash on his forehead.

Jah chuckled dryly. "I ain't gon' shoot you," he said.

He squatted down and pistol-whipped Joseph's face until the man was unconscious, then left out as if nothing had happened.

Chapter 16

Stain wasn't about to let this one slide.

He'd warned the bitch at the store. He'd told her not to fucking put her hands on his daughter. She hadn't listened, and now she was going to pay.

He and two younger guys — Martez and Jamie — had just crammed into the same row of seats in Nia's minivan. They lived across the street from him on 16th and Millard. They'd been with him last night when he fought the young punk named Jah. They'd been with him during the shootout that followed, when Stain's nephew PJ had shot D-Lo in the head.

"Muthafucka broke my baby's nose!" Stain shouted, and punched the sliding door.

"Hey, hey, hey," Nia said, turning in her seat to look at him as she stopped at a red light on Douglas. "My van ain't did shit to your baby, okay? Take that aggression out on the bitch she got into it with. Please and thank you."

"You said it was a nigga with the bitch?'

"Yeah. I tried to swing on ol' girl and the nigga pulled out a big-ass gun on me, so I stepped back."

Stain looked over at the .45-caliber semiautomatic pistol Martez had in his hand. "Nigga, you better shoot the fuck outta whoever this nigga is if we see him. You see what happened last night. We could've died if we didn't have them guns. They shot Tommy and Ray, got them all fucked up layin' in the hospital and shit. When we see these muthafuckas, I'm gon' kill the bitch who put her hands on my baby, but you better not let no nigga get off on me."

"I won't, man. You know I'm on it. I'm ready to shoot somethin' anyway," Martez replied, cocking the pistol.

Clenching his teeth together, Stain turned his eyes back to his window and waited for Nia to pull up at the building on Douglas and Homan. He kept balling and unballing his fists. He was going to beat Tirzah to death when he got his hands on her. Sharon was on the way to the hospital with a broken nose and a busted up face. The bitch who'd done it would get treated even worse.

Sharon had told him what kind of car to look for: a red Ford Taurus. It was Tirzah's sister's car. Tirzah lived on the fourth floor, in the apartment on the right.

Stain couldn't wait to get there.

They had just a few more blocks to go.

Chapter 17

"Oh, my God, Rell. Joseph's not answering his phone! If Jah did something to him..."

"Chill out. He'll be good." Rell gave Tamera a quick peck on the cheek. She was sitting on his leg again, this time at the kitchen table.

Tirzah was at the stove, overlooking the steaming pot of raviolis she'd put on a few minutes prior.

"I'm telling you now, Rell," Tamera said, "if he's done something to Joe, we're going to have big problems. I'm dead-ass serious. That's my fucking friend."

"We don't know if he did something to your friend or not. Chill the fuck out. Damn. The least you can do is wait until he gets back. Ain't no sense in accusing him of some shit already."

Tamera rolled her eyes and shook her head. Rell let his hands roam across her thighs, leaning in to give her yet another peck on the cheek.

Then he thought of something that would calm her down. "Get up right quick," he said. "I'ma show you somethin'."

He went to Big Man and Susan's bedroom and returned seconds later with the ring.

Tamera's eyes got big when she saw it. "Jesus, how many carats is that?" she said, reaching out for it. "That rock is huge. Tirzah, come over here and look at this."

Rell handed the ring to Tamera. She tried it on, and her mouth fell open.

"This is so beautiful," she said.

Rell nodded. "It's nine carats. Worth about a hundred grand. Susan left it on accident. I gotta send it to her when they get to Florida."

Tirzah tried it on next. The amazed looks on their faces made Rell smile.

"Did you know," Tamera said, "that the ring symbolizes a never-ending love? The circle of it. There is no beginning or end of a ring, you know."

"Nah, I ain't know that." Rell, too, became lost in the beautiful diamond.

"Yeah," Tamera continued, "and way back in the day, people used to believe that there was a vein in the ring finger that ran directly to the heart. It's not true, but it's a sweet idea. I've read about engagement rings. One day I wanna be married, too."

"Yeah, and so do I," Tirzah added, pulling the ring off her finger.

Tamera wanted to try it on a second time, and Rell watched her do it, studying the tremendous amount of joy in her pretty brown eyes. She seemed to be lost in some magical place that wasn't here in Big Man's dreary little apartment. Her chest expanded as she took in a breath and held her hand out to look at the ring from afar.

"It's beautiful," she said, holding one hand to her chest.

"It is," Tirzah said.

The emotional moment was ended abruptly by the sound of shattering glass.

Tirzah and Tamera's eyes went wide.

"The fuck was that?" Rell said, his brows coming together thoughtfully.

"If that bitch just did something to my car...!" Tamera said.

The three of them walked quickly to the living room window and peeked out through the blinds...just as a heavyset man in a blue jacket punched through the driver's window of Tamera's red Taurus.

"Oh, shit. That's Sharon's daddy," Tirzah said. "He's busting out your windows."

"Yeah, no shit, Sherlock," Tamera snapped.

"Damn." Rell shook his head and let out a sigh. "Come on, Tamera. Tirzah, you keep your ass in here," he said, and headed for the door.

King Rio

Chapter 18

Stain had a towel he'd found in the back of Nia's minivan wrapped around the fist he was using to punch out the car windows.

He knew the names of the three boys who were standing on the corner selling heroin. They were Lil Zo, Chris, and E, and all three of them were laughing and cheering him on.

He wasn't in the laughing mood. In fact, he wanted to walk over to them and show them just how funny his punches were.

"This makes a lot of sense, Stain," Nia said, holding her hips and shaking her head at him. "We know what apartment the bitch is in. Why not just go up there? You're wasting time and energy smashing windows and shit."

Gritting his teeth, Stain waved for Martez and Jamie to come with him as he headed up the porch stairs and into the apartment building.

He was fuming, angrier than he'd ever been. The image of his daughter's battered face was still fresh in his mind. He had just pulled up with the guys when she came stumbling out of Nia's minivan, sobbing uncontrollably and holding her bloodied nose.

"Daddy, that bitch beat me up!" she'd said, and Nia had immediately volunteered to take him to Tirzah's apartment.

The staircase had a dank, moldy smell to it. A group of young teenagers were hunched over just inside the door, rolling dice and smoking weed.

Stain stormed up the wooden stairs, fighting the urge to punch the wall as he went. He shoved past a thuggishly dressed young man on the second floor and received a few cuss words because of it.

He was making his way up the stairs to the third floor when he came face to face with a light-skinned man and a beautiful brown-skinned woman.

The man looked strangely familiar.

So did the girl. It took Stain a couple of seconds to realize that he'd seen her walking out of Anna's earlier, right after he'd checked the Tirzah bitch.

"Ay, I can't have all that drama in my building," the young man said. "You can't be busting out car windows and shit. If you got a problem with a nigga, catch him in the streets, not in here."

Stain's nostrils flared. "Stay the fuck outta my business, and get the fuck outta my way. Where's that bitch Tirzah? You know her? Tell her to get her ass out here and fight me. She wanna be Ronda Rousey, tell that bitch Floyd Mayweather out here ready to give her li'l hoodrat ass a real fight."

Martez said, "I'd advise y'all to move." He had his head ducked deep in his bright yellow hoodie, and his hands were in the hoodie's belly pocket, no doubt holding his gun. Behind him Jamie wore a similar hoodie, only it was gray with a small rip in the left shoulder.

Stain nodded. "I think you might wanna listen to my li'l homie. This ain't what you want. Not today it ain't."

Chapter 19

"A'ight, a'ight. Calm down, my nigga. It ain't even that serious," Rell said, raising his hands in surrender and taking two steps back. He mumbled to Tamera, "Baby, get back. This nigga's serious."

The look on Tamera's face said it all: she was pissed that the man had smashed out her car windows. Reluctantly, she backed up with Rell, hands planted on her wide hips, scowling at the man.

"Damn, right, I'm serious," the big guy said.

Rell had taken the steps back for a good reason. He'd noticed that Jah was coming up the stairs behind the three men.

As soon as the guy in the yellow hoodie made it to the top stair, Rell punched him as hard as he could in the chin and sent him tumbling backward down the stairs. He landed unconscious at Jah's feet, and Jah hopped right over him, drawing his gun from inside his leather jacket and taking aim at the guy in the gray hoodie.

Rell pulled his gun from his hip, grabbed the back of the big guy's jacket, and snatched him down to the hallway floor. He pushed the gun barrel in the angry man's eye.

"Get the fuck up outta here, nigga! I asked you nicely the first time!" Rell shouted in the man's face.

Jah said, "Bruh, that's the nigga I got into it with last night! That's Stain!" He made Gray Hoodie lay down on the floor and then aimed his gun at Stain.

"Nah, bruh. Not here," Rell said quickly.

Jah became furious in a matter of seconds. He walked up the last few stairs, pointing the Ruger at Stain's face.

"Nah, bruh," Rell repeated, just as Tirzah appeared at the top of the stairs on the fourth floor.

Jah wore an expression of pure rage. He was almost snarling as he stood over Stain, his gun trained on the older man's forehead.

The gunshots were incredibly loud.

But they didn't come from Jah's gun.

Rell grabbed Jah's shoulder and shoved him onto the stairs leading up to the fourth floor as the guy in the yellow hoodie staggered to his feet, firing off poorly aimed rounds as he fell against the wall.

The next five seconds seemed to go in slow-motion.

Jah got up, reached over the railing with his Ruger in hand, and returned fire.

Instinctively, Rell gave Tamera a push that sent her slamming into the door of apartment 3A.

His quick thinking wasn't really needed.

He saw the guy in the yellow hoodie's head jerk to the side as one of Jah's bullets hit him on the top left side of his head. He saw the blood and brain matter splatter on the wall to the right of the man.

Yellow Hoodie fell against the same wall a half second later.

Stain and Gray Hoodie got up and just about flew down the stairs. Jah sent three shots at them as they fled, but all of the rounds hit the wall at the foot of the stairs on the second floor.

All eight eyes — Tirzah's, Jah's, Tamera's, and Rell's — were wide open during the following couple of minutes.

Rell went upstairs and locked the door to his father's apartment before returning to the crime scene.

Then the four of them rushed out of the building and into his Impala.

The young guys on the corner stared in through the windshield as Rell turned his key in the ignition. With Douglas being a boulevard, with houses and apartment buildings on both sides, there were dozens of eyewitnesses, all of them gazing at the Impala as Rell sped off and veered around the corner onto Homan.

He hoped none of them would talk to the cops when they arrived.

After all, there was a dead body in his father's building, which he'd been left in charge of for the next two weeks.

Chapter 20

"You saved that hoe-ass nigga," Jah complained from the backseat. "They killed D-Lo, bruh. I got in a fight with dude, too. I was supposed to off that nigga."

Rell shook his head no. He had both hands on the steering wheel. He was on Kedzie, with no real idea of where he was going.

Next to him, Tamera was downloading a police scanner app on her smartphone. She'd said that one of her friends had gotten away from the cops using it in the past. Rell didn't quite understand her logic, but he wasn't going to question it. His only goal now was to get Jah out of Chicago, far away from the murder he'd just committed.

"I'm about to get on the highway," Rell said, feeling nervous as he drove past the police station.

"You sure picked the right street to drive down," Jah commented.

"Shut up talkin' to me, li'l dude."

"I'm just sayin', nigga. Why in the fuck is you ridin' past the police station? Kinda sense that make?"

Tamera laughed. Rell glanced over at her and said, "You can shut up, too. You ain't special."

Tirzah said, "Jah's right. You shouldn't have stopped him from poppin' Stain's punk ass. Stain killed his friend, and the nigga was comin' for me. Fuck him. He deserved to get whacked. If I had a gun I would've done it myself."

"You wouldn't have done a goddamn thing." Rell turned on the radio and turned up the volume. Drake's "Back to Back" was playing on Power 92:

Yeah, I learned the game from William Wesley
You can never check me

Back to back for the niggas that didn't get the message
Back to back like I'm on the cover of Lethal Weapon...

The music served its purpose.

Everyone got quiet, giving Rell the time he needed to think.

It took him about two minutes to make up his mind. He had well over $5,000 in his pocket. First he would get a hotel room. Then he would talk Jah into getting rid of the murder weapon. He'd buy Jah another gun if that's what it took.

As soon as the song ended, Tirzah reached an arm forward between the front seats and lowered the volume.

"Everybody listen," she said. "I have an idea. A damned good one, too." When no one spoke, she continued. "Stain has a nephew from down south. A nigga named PJ. Tamera, you know PJ. The nigga with the black Tahoe, the one who came to Jessie's birthday party last summer with all that jewelry on. Anyway, he got big money. Long money. We should rob his ass. His house caught fire a couple days ago. He moved in with some bitch on 16th and St. Louis. We might be able to come up outta there with forty or fifty thousand. Probably three or four bricks, too. I'm telling you, it's the lick."

Rell nodded his head at the idea as he stopped at the corner of Kedzie Avenue and Augusta Boulevard, right at the entrance to Humboldt Park. He'd heard of PJ during his prison bid, but never had met the guy.

The strong scent of some loud-smelling weed threw off his thoughts. He lifted his nose and sniffed.

"I smell it, too," Tamera said.

Rell looked back at Jah. "What happened to my half-ounce?"

"Yeah," Tamera said, "and what happened when you got to Joseph's house?"

Jah chuckled. "I got the weed in the trunk. That shit smells so good it's coming through the seats."

"No." Tamera shook her head. "A half-ounce of Kush ain't gonna smell that damn loud."

"Who said it was a half-ounce? How you know he didn't show us some love and throw in a li'l extra?"

Tamera squinted her eyes at Jah. She spoke in a low, serious tone. "If you did some fucked up shit to my friend..."

"Stop accusing me of shit. You don't even know what the fuck went down. Damn, nigga. Chill the fuck out. Turn the mu'fuckin' music back up or somethin'."

Sucking her teeth, Tamera turned to Rell and said, "I can already tell your brother is going to be getting on my nerves every single day."

A smirk grew on Rell's face. He parked, popped the trunk, and told Jah to grab the weed. He waited for Jah to get out of the car before he said anything else.

"We're about to smoke and then head to the mall to eat and do a little shoppin'. I ain't got much to spend, but I'll get us all something. Think of it as a Christmas gift. When we leave the mall, we'll go out to a movie or somethin', then we can get a hotel room for the night. I'll go back to the building tomorrow morning to see what's up. Y'all cool with that?"

"I can't believe that shit just went down," Tamera said, looking down at the ring on her finger.

Rell hadn't realized that he had not gotten the ring back until now. It looked good on Tamera's slender brown finger. The diamond glistened beautifully in the sunlight. Staring at it brought a brief, two-second smile to Tamera's face.

Then the trunk slammed shut, and Jah returned to his seat. The front of his jacket was bulging out like a pregnant woman's belly.

He unzipped the jacket and lifted out two large bags of Kush.

Tamera gasped. "You son of a bitch. You robbed him, didn't you? You fucking robbed him."

"Got Hawaiian Kush," Jah said, smiling brightly and ignoring Tamera, "and some kinda light green Kush. I bought him out."

Tirzah laughed. "He did not give you all that for a hundred dollars. You can cancel that lie."

There was no time to argue about how Jah had acquired the Kush. Rell took a handful out of the bag that had the orangeish Kush and made Jah put the rest of it back in the trunk. Then he drove off, on his way to a gas station to fill up his tank and get some blunts.

He turned on Drake and Future's new mixtape and skipped to "30 for 30" before turning the volume back up.

The music kept Tamera from arguing with Jah.

Chapter 21

Never thought I'd be talking from this perspective
But I'm not really sure what else you expected
When the higher-ups have all come together as a collective
With conspiracies to end my run and send me a message...

Stain was only half listening to the Drake song that was blaring from his nephew PJ's SUV at the curb.

Standing on the porch of the redbrick house he rented on 16th and Millard with an AK-47 assault rifle and a 12-gauge shotgun laying at his feet, Stain's eyes were flicking every which way. He was itching to pick up the assault rifle and open fire on a fuck nigga.

Jamie was sitting in the flashy SUV with PJ, smoking some weed in memory of Martez. The policemen who'd been heckling everyone on Millard about last night's shooting were now gone, and Stain guessed they were at the building on Douglas.

There was a crowd of young men and women in Stain's living room. A lot of them were shedding tears for Martez. Bottles of liquor and blunts were being passed around. Peaches, Stain's girlfriend, was in the kitchen cooking a big meal for their visitors.

Precious, Martez's sister, was present. So were two of his cousins and a few of his best friends.

Stain was grinding his teeth together. He couldn't believe that little motherfucker Jah had ruined his day again. It was Jah's fist that had his eye swollen. His jaw hurt like hell where Jah had punched him twice during their fight. His back was aching where Jah had landed another vicious punch.

"I am going to kill that li'l nigga as soon as I get my hands on him," Stain said aloud to himself.

He licked his chapped lips and rubbed a hand down his face, trying to decide if he should go and sit in the Tahoe with PJ and Jamie or go in the house with the grieving crew of youngsters.

He picked up the AK-47 and rushed down the stairs, on his way to join PJ and Jamie.

Today was not his lucky day.

He slipped on a bit of slush on the bottom stair and landed hard on his hip and elbow.

"Goddamnit!" He let out a miserable groan and winced in pain. "I'm going to fucking kill you, Jah. Young punk. Your ass is mine when I catch up with you."

He realized that he was blaming Jah for the fall, but he didn't care. Maybe it really was Jah's fault. Maybe Jah had somehow cursed him. His life had gone to shit ever since the fight with Jah. First, the young punk had almost knocked him out. If not for a lucky uppercut Stain had managed to land, he knew he'd have lost the fight. And if PJ hadn't been around the corner when Jah's crew came back for a gunfight, he knew he would be dead instead of lying on ass with an aching back and elbow on this cold, sunny December afternoon.

Peaches was pissed off about the fight and the shooting that had taken the life of Jah's friend. She knew that PJ had been the shooter, but that didn't matter. As far as she was concerned, it was all Stain's fault, which explained why she hadn't given him any of the good stuff last night or this morning. And now, with Martez dead and a houseful of sad faces, he doubted if tonight and tomorrow morning would be any different.

PJ stuck his head out of the driver's window and laughed.

"I hear you out there cussin' out ghosts and shit. Old ass."

"Fuck you too, li'l nigga." Stain was in no mood to joke around. His entire body was killing him.

He dusted off the snow and slush from his jacket and jeans and then got in the backseat of PJ's fly SUV. It was one of those Chevy trucks with the big rims and ridiculously loud speakers that shook the whole neighborhood. The seats were brown leather. The exterior paint was chameleon, changing from purple to green to blue to yellow every time Stain looked at it. The dashboard and steering wheel were made of wood-grain. There were televisions in the front and back of the head-rests and on the inside of the doors. It was all much more than Stain would ever waste money on, even if he had the kind of money PJ had.

He set down the assault rifle and massaged his elbow.

PJ turned the rearview mirror to Stain's face. "You a'ight back there, old man? Looked like a hard fall you took."

"Don't start with me, PJ. I ain't in the mood. We need to be—"

Stain paused as a Chicago police car came flying up Millard. It jumped the curb at the corner where two young boys were standing, and seconds later, the two policemen had them with their hands in the air as they experienced a roughly administered pat-down.

Pushing the AK-47 down to the floor, Stain said, "Ain't this about a bitch."

"Nigga," PJ said, "didn't nobody ask your smart ass to bring the K off the porch in the first mu'fuckin' place. Come on, let's go in the crib. And leave that on the floor, smart guy."

"Shut up."

PJ was a tall, huge man, as dark as the night, with no neck and a mouthful of gold teeth. He'd been born and raised in Atlanta until his mom passed away when he was seventeen. Then he'd come to Chicago and stayed with Stain until he turned eighteen and moved into his own place out south. Since then, PJ had managed to have seven kids by five different women. Stain knew it was because of PJ's money. There was some guy PJ knew from Atlanta who kept him with some of the best heroin in the city.

Just looking at PJ as he waddled his way out of the Tahoe, it was easy to see that he had money. From the gold rings on his fingers to the fresh black fur coat on his back and the Gucci shades over his eyes, everything about him said money. Stain could not help but to feel a bit of jealousy at how good PJ was living. He felt that PJ owed him some of that drug money for taking him in years earlier. He could have easily left the black bastard out in the cold. The least PJ could do was throw him about $20,000 to set him straight.

They moved quickly to the porch and up the stairs. Stain was careful to avoid the treacherous bottom step this time.

He led them into the house and straight to his bedroom where he knew they wouldn't be bothered by the youngsters.

"Turn on some music, Unc," PJ said, digging in a box of Little Debbie cakes on the side of the bed. "Not none of that old shit, either. I ain't tryna hear no James Brown."

"Nigga, that's ya problem. James Brown is classic music for black folks. That mess you young niggas listen to now ain't no damn music. You wouldn't know good music if it slapped you in the face."

"If you turn on some James Brown, I'm gon' slap you in the face." PJ fell over laughing as he ripped open the wrapper of his treat and bit into the cake. "Man, I gotta get back out south. The law just be pullin' up outta nowhere out this way. They scared to pull that kinda shit on the south side. Them li'l niggas ain't goin'. They out there shootin' at everything movin'. I ain't on that shit. I'm just tryna get me some money."

PJ acted as if he hadn't murdered a teenager in cold blood last night.

After turning on the dusty old stereo system and tuning it to a hip hop station, Stain went to the twenty-dollar bag of heroin he had on the dresser and snorted a line while PJ lit another blunt for him and Jamie. Stain wasn't a heroin addict, in his opinion. He was just an occasional user. Once or twice a day was enough for him. Most of the time he could go a whole day without using. It all depended on his mood, if Peaches was bugging him or not.

He was on his second line when someone knocked at the door.

"Yeah? Who is it?" Stain said.

"It's Tasha. I think I have some information you might wanna know."

Tasha was Martez's girlfriend. Well, she used to be Martez's girlfriend.

Stain went to the door and cracked it open. He looked out at Tasha and immediately felt bad for her. "What is it?"

"I know where Jah lives," she said, wiping tears from her eyes. "He stays with his momma on Avers. I can take y'all to the house."

Chapter 22

The orange Kush was better than Rell had expected. It was so good that he got lazy and instantly changed his mind about going shopping and going to a hotel. Instead, he drove to Mama's three-bedroom house on 13th and Avers.

Maria was asleep on the couch when he walked in with Tamera at his side. Jah and Tirzah stayed out front with a group of his friends.

There was a half empty bottle of Seagram's gin beside an ashtray on the carpet near Maria's head. Dora, Jah's newborn daughter, was sleeping in a swing next to the sofa. *Scandal* was playing on the TV.

Tamera snickered as Rell led the way to his bedroom.

"What's so funny?" he asked.

"She's out of it," Tamera said.

"You can get off my OG."

"I'm not making fun of her. Just saying. She looks like she went to sleep feeling good. I need some of what she had."

"Bullshit. You think you do." Rell unlocked his door, pushed it open, and stepped aside to let Tamera in first.

The bedroom hadn't changed much since his teenage years. He still had the same twin bed he'd gotten for his fifteenth birthday, though the red sheets and pillows were brand-new. The walls were off-white from back when he and Jah had painted them a few years back. He had a bunch of shoeboxes stacked in his closet, each one containing a pair of shoes that he kept as clean as possible. Scattered around his TV were DVD cases, mostly porn. The same old CD player he'd had since high school was on his dresser, and stacked up beside it were rap and R&B CDs, though he rarely listened to them. On the windowsill was an ashtray full of blunt roaches and two bullets that went to the .45-caliber Smith and Wesson he'd had before he went to prison.

Tamera sat down on the foot of the bed while Rell locked the door. He went straight to his dresser and pulled out the top drawer.

Underneath a pile of T-shirts he had a 30-shot clip for the .40-caliber Glock on his hip. He took the 16-round magazine out of his Glock and slid in the 30-round.

Tamera shook her head, but she didn't say a word. The incident at the apartment building on Douglas called for drastic measures, and Rell could see the approval in her eyes. Like him, she just wanted to be safe.

He put the gun on his dresser, turned on the CD player, pressed play on a 90's R&B album, and took off his sweatshirt as Shai's "If I Ever Fall In Love Again" started. Studying himself in the mirror, he ran a thumb and a forefinger across his eyebrows.

"Oh, please." Tamera cracked up laughing. "You know you need to stop. Who you think you is, Chris Brown? Boy, if you don't sit down somewhere."

"Quit frontin'. You love this face," Rell said, biting his bottom lip and looking at her reflection.

Her eyes went to the ring on her finger.

"Hope you know I need that back," Rell said.

"I know. It's just so beautiful. God, I hope I get proposed to with a ring like this one day. I'm going to dislocate my jaw on that man."

"Dislocate your jaw?" Rell turned around to face her. "What you mean by that?"

"I mean just what I said."

"You gon' make me marry you just to see what that's like." He chuckled once.

"I might marry you for that tongue action you gave me," Tamera countered, smiling.

Rell walked to her with a middle finger raised. She rolled her eyes up until she felt his lips on her neck. He kissed her there, then pecked his way up to her mouth and sucked on her lower lip.

"I need a good girl in my life," he murmured. "Tired of hoes."

"I'm most definitely not a hoe. Haven't fucked a nigga since Kendrick went to jail, and I don't even fuck with him no more."

"So, it's us?"

"That's up to you, Rell."

"If it's up to me" —he planted another kiss on her lips— "then that's what it is. Take this shit off." He curled his fingers in the waistline of her sweatpants and underwear and peeled them down in one quick motion.

"You can't just be D-Bo on my pussy like that. Make me question what you really went to prison for." Tamera's alluring smile and sweet giggle followed.

"You tryna call me a rapist?"

"I don't know."

"Well," Rell said, throwing her legs in the air, "I'ma take it right now, then."

"Go right ahead."

The Hawaiian Kush had left Rell's mouth cotton-dry, but now it watered in anticipation of the taste of Tamera's pussy. He'd loved the taste of it earlier, and he knew that here, in his own bedroom, he'd love it even more. Here he was in his element. He'd always liked the taste of pussy before he went away, but he hadn't put his mouth on one since he came home. Not that he hadn't wanted to. It was just that he wasn't going to lick on just any woman, and Erica was far too slutty to even think about eating her pussy.

Tamera was a different story.

He dug his tongue in as far as it would go before going up to flicker it on her clitoris. She tasted delicious.

He gripped her meaty thighs in his hands and pressed his face snugly into her juicy lower lips, licking and sucking, spitting and slurping. Her fingertips dug in his scalp. Her gasps became moans. She winded her hips and humped his face.

"You like that shit?" he said, and went back to sucking on her clit.

His dick became as hard as a brick in his pants. The scrumptious scent of Tamera's pussy — combined with the soulful crooning of Shai — made him suck and lick even harder.

If I say that I could be your one and only
Promise that you'll never leave me lonely
I just wanna be the one you need, oh baby...

By the end of the song, Tamera was trembling in orgasm and her juices were dripping from Rell's chin. He went on licking. She tasted too good to stop. The look of ecstasy on her face compelled him to keep going. She grabbed one of his pillows and put it over her face to mute the scream that came immediately afterward.

It was the scream that stopped him.

Smiling widely, he stood up and dropped his pants and boxers for the second time today. This time, however, he didn't put on a condom, because he didn't have another one.

Either Tamera didn't notice or she didn't care. She merely put her hands on his ribs and gasped as he sank all the way in and began thrusting.

He'd left her sweats and underwear around her ankles, and now they made for a nice makeshift handle as he used it to hold her legs up and off to the side.

He looked down at his dick, almost hypnotized by the sight of Tamera's juices on it as he slid in and out, in and out, in and out.

New Edition's "Can You Stand The Rain" played loudly behind him, but he could still hear the squishy wet sounds. If not for his mother being asleep in the living room, he would turn off the music just to hear the euphonious sounds of their sex.

He lowered his mouth to Tamera's full lips and sucked and kissed on them. She couldn't return the kisses. Her mouth was wide open, face twisted, eyes agape. She was moaning incessantly.

Her sex faces were so beautiful, Rell noticed. He could look at them all day and night.

A couple of minutes passed before he decided to end the Mr. Nice Guy act. He started pounding her with piston-like speed.

She lifted her hips up off the bed and dug her fingernails in his back. Her mouth and eyes opened wider. A single tear escaped her left eye and rolled down into her ear.

The snugness of her pussy had Rell ready to cum in no time. Just when he felt the familiar sensation in his scrotum, he pulled out of her and slapped the head of his thick love stick on her clit until the feeling passed.

He got on the bed and lay next to her. "Get on top, baby," he said, and kissed her on the cheek.

"Wait a second. My legs are numb right now." She giggled sweetly and exhaled heavily. For the umpteenth time, she raised her hand and looked at the ring. "That was some hundred-thousand-dollar head you gave me. I'd take that over a ring any day."

"Fuck you." Rell was still smiling. He pushed a forefinger in her cheek, stroking his dick in the other hand. "Hurry up."

With a sigh and a roll of the eyes, she got up, kicking off her sweats and underwear, and mounted him. She held his dick in place as she slowly lowered herself down onto it.

Rell put his hands on her ass and assisted her in setting a rhythmic bounce. He pumped upward every time she came down. Thinking back to the girls he'd bedded in the past, he could not think of one with a pussy as tight and wet as Tamera's. She had that snapback, the kind of pussy that turned unsuspecting men into fathers. Her facial expressions were as sexy as her moans. She took off her hoodie and T-shirt, and Rell's hands immediately went to her breasts. They were small and perky, C-cups, by the looks of them, just enough to fill Rell's hands. He sat up and sucked on the nipples, but only for a minute or so. Then he eased back and let Tamera ride him like a madwoman.

Chapter 23

The sun was going down.

Maria's home was on the first floor of a two-story red-brick duplex building that Big Man had been trying to buy for the past year. It stood between two nearly identical buildings directly across the street from Henson Elementary School.

Although there was a ton of snow, the temperature wasn't freezing like it had been earlier in the day.

There were close to thirty teenagers and adults standing outside in front of Maria's house, all of them wearing hoodies or jackets, gloves, and boots. A few girls wore scarves. Their cups were for the most part full of liquor, though a number of them were drinking Lean.

The guys had guns stashed everywhere: inside their jackets and under their hoodies, beneath cars, in a flower pot on Maria's front porch, in the gangway next to Maria's building. Even a couple of the girls were strapped.

Johnny B and Lil Larry had already gotten "RIP D-Lo" on the fronts of their hoodies. They had dreadlocks and, like Jah, they toted pistols with extended clips.

Everyone was celebrating in D-Lo's memory, and already many of them were calling 13th and Avers "D-Block" in honor of Darius "D-Lo" Wallace.

"D-Block, bitch!" Jah shouted at two passing cars. He was sitting on the trunk of the Impala, rolling a blunt of the Hawaiian Kush while Tirzah stood in front of him with the fifth of Hennessy he'd just had one of the girls buy for him during a run to the liquor store.

"You got me out here with all these thirsty-ass niggas," Tirzah whispered to him. "That ugly nigga with the dreads keeps walking past to look at my ass. These hoes got jealousy all in their eyes. I ain't feeling this shit."

"You got a fat ass," Jah reasoned, "and you a bad bitch. Niggas gon' look. Hoes gon' be jealous. You gotta expect that kinda shit. At least you ain't ugly and dusty. You got your hair done, nails done. You the shit. Fuck a hater. Let 'em keep lookin'."

"I bet Rell and Tamera are in there gettin' it in while we're out here freezing our asses off."

Jah shrugged, licking the blunt closed. "Shit, they might be. I ain't freezin'."

"Well, I am."

"A'ight, gimme twenty minutes out here with the guys. Then we can go in. That cool with you?"

"I guess."

"Good. Now keep your eyes on the street. Look at the cars behind me, and at anybody walkin' up. Just in case I don't see somethin' I'm supposed to see. You gotta be my second set of eyes."

"You'll be fine as long as I'm with you," Tirzah promised. "I know how shit goes out here. I know how to watch out for my man."

"Your man?" Jah raised his brows. "Is that what I am now? Your man?"

"Nigga, I sucked your dick, so you're my man. Why, is that a problem?" Chuckling at the absurdity of her words, Tirzah turned up the bottle and took a big gulp of the cognac.

Jah chuckled right along with her. He'd stuffed about an ounce of the Hawaiian Kush in a baggie and handed it to Tirzah to roll up for the gang, but once she'd mentioned that he could easily make $400 off every ounce, he'd changed his mind and told her to keep it in her purse. She rolled a blunt for herself while he lit his and passed it to Johnny B.

"Man," Johnny B said, "they say the law over there deep as fuck at Pimpin' Dave's building. You talked to your pops?"

"Nah." Jah blew a stream of smoke in the sky. "The law over there because of me. I caught up wit' dude n'em. The niggas who whacked D-Lo. Got one of 'em out the way. Tried to get that nigga I fought, but he ran up outta there so mu'fuckin' fast I couldn't get him. Nigga outran the bullets."

"It's all good. We finna slide down on Millard in a few minutes. First nigga we see gets it, on Neal. I know where the nigga Stain live. He's a dopefiend, lord. The nigga done bought bags from us before."

"I can't go over there," Jah said, taking the bottle from Tirzah as she leaned back against him. "They'll be lookin' for me to slide on 'em. You better believe they got just as many guns as we do right now."

Johnny B shrugged dismissively, passing the blunt back to Jah. "I don't give a fuck if they got a thousand guns. I'm lettin' this whole thirty go soon as we hit the corner. Ain't no nigga gon' whack one of the guys and not get a war behind it. On Neal, I'm willin' to die 'bout that."

Jah was in complete agreement with Johnny B. D-Lo had been one of their best friends since grammar school. There was no way his death would go unavenged.

Tirzah turned to face Jah, and out of respect for their privacy, Johnny B took a few steps back.

"How old are you?" she asked.

"Old enough," Jah said.

"I'm serious."

"You think I ain't?" He drank from the bottle. "Nah, I'm seventeen. I'll be eighteen on March first. Rell's birthday is February first."

"I am going to jail. Child molestation. Do you know I'm twenty-six? I'm almost ten years older than you."

"And? What the fuck that's supposed to mean?" Jah rubbed Tirzah's big butt and gave it a sharp slap, gazing down at her beautiful face as she stared up at him with her back arched in the sexiest pose. "I'm grown, li'l momma. I take care of myself. I buy my own clothes. I take care of my daughter. I do more than most of these forty-year-old niggas do for their babies."

"Don't take it like that. I'm not saying you don't provide for yours. I'm just saying, there's a lot you have to learn. At seventeen, I was stripping."

"Damn, you used to be a stripper?"

"Don't get any ideas."

"I wanna see what that mu'fucka do." Jah showed a beaming smile.

Tirzah rolled her eyes and turned her back to him, but he kept his arms wrapped around her.

In his opinion, he'd struck gold with Tirzah. She was just as pretty as Tamera and twice as thick. Plus, Jah loved redbones, and Tirzah was as bad as redbones came.

He had the Ruger on his lap. Tirzah glanced at the gun and shook her head, but she didn't speak on it.

Suddenly, one of the guys suggested that now was the perfect time to pay the Conservative Vice Lords on Millard a visit. Everyone agreed that Jah should stay home. He'd put in work last night, wounding several of the CVLs. He'd earned the right to sit this one out.

He watched the gang as they climbed in their cars and zoomed off down the street, leaving behind mostly girls to hang out with Jah and Tirzah.

Jah got fucked up off the Hennessey, so wasted that he found himself sucking and kissing on Tirzah's neck just a few minutes later.

"You're drunk, Jah. Come on, let's go inside. You said give you twenty minutes; it's been almost an hour."

Getting down from the trunk of his big brother's car, Jah forgot all about his gun until he heard it clatter to the street.

"See what I mean?" Tirzah said, shaking her head. "You're out here dumb-drunk in the middle of the night, and a war has just started. This is not the time to be off your square."

Jah tried reaching down for the gun and ended up stumbling several feet away. Sucking her teeth, Tirzah grabbed ahold of his jacket and held it until he regained his balance.

Then she squatted down to pick up his gun...just as a white car came creeping up through the alley behind Maria's building.

King Rio

Chapter 24

They were in a Chevy Lumina that PJ had paid a heroin addict two $20 bags of the good stuff to use for the night.

Ducked low in the backseat next to Jamie, Stain had the AK-47 cradled in his hands. He was immensely nervous, but he knew that he was ready to go through with this. He had to put an end to Jah before Jah put an end to him.

PJ said, "I think that's...yeah, that's him right there. Right out front. Look like he drunk or somethin'. Hurry up, nigga. Get out there and handle that shit before they peep us sittin' back here."

Stain took in a deep, relaxing breath. He'd never killed a man in his entire forty-four years of living, and he wasn't quite sure he was ready to do it now, but he didn't have much of a choice. Last night after his fistfight with Jah, the young guy had come back with an assault rifle and shot two of the CVLs who'd been standing outside with Stain. A few of the bullets had actually come so close to hitting him that he'd felt the searing heat of them flying past.

His back and elbow were still aching from the fall he'd taken earlier. His nerves were still rattled from seeing Martez get his brains blown out.

"You ready?" Jamie said. He was holding the shotgun.

Stain took another breath and gave a nod. "Yeah. Come on."

He pushed open his door — the rear passenger side door — and pushed one leg out, then the other.

Another deep breath.

Jamie pushed open the other rear door.

Then the most unexpected thing happened.

The back door of the house they were parked behind swung open, and the guy who'd pushed the barrel of a gun in

Stain's eye just before Jah killed Martez came running out of the house, aiming a gun with a long clip at the Lumina.

Stain's eyes widened in horror. He didn't even get a chance to raise the AK-47 before the gun in the young man's hand started barking.

He felt the bullets hitting his legs, stomach, and chest as PJ sped off down the alley, and the last thing he saw before a round pierced his skull was the girl who'd beat up his daughter.

She was running up from the gangway next to the house, firing a gun that looked exactly like the one the boy was firing.

Then a bullet hit Stain in the side of his head, and he ceased to exist.

Chapter 25

Rell was surprised to see Tirzah come from the side of the house shooting Jah's gun, but he had no time to pay her any mind. He was far too focused on trying to kill every person in the fleeing car.

He'd seen the headlights turning into the alley through his bedroom window, and after seeing who was in the backseat he had wasted no time grabbing his gun off the dresser and rushing to the back door with it, which explained why he was outside shirtless in the middle of the winter.

Stain was Rell's first victim. He was just stepping out of the car, and the guy in the gray hoodie was coming around the rear of the car holding a shotgun when Rell took aim and let Stain have it.

BOOM! BOOM! BOOM! BOOM! BOOM! BOOM! BOOM!

The gunshots seemed to frighten Gray Hoodie. He let off one stentorian blast from the shotgun and then took off running as the car sped off in the other direction with Stain's legs hanging out the open door.

Since Tirzah was still shooting at the car, Rell turned his attention to Gray Hoodie. He ran after him down the dark, cold alley. It was a short run. He aimed and sent four shots, and one of them knocked Gray Hoodie to the ground. He fell flat on his stomach and started crawling. Rell jogged up on him, glancing back just as the white car zoomed out of the other end of the alley.

"Come on, lord. This ain't for us," Gray Hoodie pleaded as he continued to crawl.

Rell shot him in the lower back and smiled as he fell flat to the ground.

"You niggas came to murk my li'l brother? You thought it was gon' be sweet?" He kicked the guy over onto his back.

Eyes that were replete with fear looked up at Rell. The man coughed up a mouthful of blood. For some odd reason he lifted his arms, reaching out to Rell.

"Nuh uh, nigga. It's over," Rell said, and squeezed the trigger twice more, sending one bullet through the man's nose and another through his forehead.

Chapter 26

Susan was in fairly good shape for a woman her age. At fifty-seven, she still exercised regularly at a gym that wasn't far from her and Big Man's apartment building, and quite often she found herself moving around furniture and lifting heavy objects without the help of her husband. She was slim and toned. Her wise gray eyes weren't what they used to be, but she rarely wore her glasses. Unlike Big Man, Susan had no children (except for Life, the cat, whom she called her son). Donovan Webster, her previous husband, had wanted kids, and he'd believed that the two of them were trying to make babies all the way up to the day a heart attack at work sent him to his grave at the age of fifty-four, but the truth was, Susan had been taking birth control pills the entire time. She didn't want kids. In fact, she'd never wanted kids. What she wanted was money and peace, and the $550,000 life insurance policy she'd had on Donovan had given her exactly that. Sometimes she questioned why she'd gone on to marry again. She was financially stable, and she'd been perfectly content with living out the rest of her days traveling the world.

She had met Big Man at a Bears game four years ago, back when she lived alone in a townhouse she'd owned at the time in Peoria, Illinois. They had small-talked about Jay Cutler for most of the game and eventually he had offered his number and a dinner date the next evening.

The rest was history. Ever since their first date, hardly a day had gone by without them being in each other's presence. They had started flipping houses together and making money hand over fist mere weeks after their first date. Just recently they had purchased a foreclosed suburban home for $98,000, and after over $100,000 in renovations and property taxes, they'd sold it to a well-known attorney for $385,000.

Together, Susan and Big Man had just over $920,000 in their joint bank account, which is why Susan could not understand why Big Man had them staying in the cramped little apartment on Douglas Boulevard in Chicago. She knew that he wanted to be near his sons, but to Susan, that wasn't a good enough reason.

She brought it up as they were on their way to the Aretha Franklin concert in Miami.

"Look at how beautiful it is down here. This is where we're supposed to be living, Dave. Not in that little bitty old apartment in Chicago," Susan said, crossing her arms and pouting.

Big Man was driving the matte black Bentley coupe he'd rented for their two-week vacation. He looked over at her and chuckled.

"I'm not kidding, David. Not kidding at all. You're babying those boys. And if you ask me, you really shouldn't have given him all that money to watch our apartment for two weeks. That just makes no sense to me."

"He's my son," Big Man argued. "I'll give him what I want, when I want. You're lucky he's there to watch over the place. If not for him, that damned ring might be gone by now. You didn't think of that, did you?"

Susan turned away from him and gazed out her window. The Bentley was lancing down Biscayne Boulevard. They were headed to the Bayfront Park Amphitheatre for the concert.

"I bet you'd be upset if you lost that ring," Big Man went on. "Bet you wouldn't be complaining about me paying Rell if it came up missing."

"If my ring comes up missing, you're buying me another one."

"Like hell I am. If that insurance doesn't cover it, you are shit out of luck. I was a fool paying a hundred grand for a single piece of jewelry anyway."

"Don't make this a bad night for me, Dave. This is supposed to be a vacation."

Big Man shrugged his massive shoulders. He wore a triumphant grin that only served to further irritate Susan.

She thought of the $450,000 life insurance policy she had on him and hoped she'd live to see it.

As he drove, Susan eyed the mark on her finger where her ring usually shined and prayed that nothing would happen to it. She loved the ring more than she loved Big Man, and she'd let him know it more than once. To her, the ring symbolized more than an unending, undying love. It also symbolized beauty in an ugly world of hateful people, wealth in a world full of poor folks. As a kid in her hometown of Birmingham, Alabama, Susan had dreamed of one day having such a large rock on her finger, though she had anticipated it being presented to her by a strikingly handsome man with washboard abs and the face of a model. The ring she got from her first husband had nothing on the one Big Man had given her. The first ring had been small and inexpensive, hardly worth the box was it presented to her in, but Big Man's ring had stunned her into saying yes. It had been love at first sight. Nine carats of pure heaven.

"Call that boy of yours," Susan said, "and give him the address to our hotel. I want my ring back by noontime tomorrow. No exceptions."

"Tomorrow's Christmas. No mail. You'll have to wait at least another day or so. Relax, honey. You'll get your ring soon enough."

Susan crossed her frail arms over her chest and pouted.

Chapter 27

When Tamera Lyon awoke the following morning, she sat up in bed and rubbed her eyes and waited for the dream to end. This had to be a dream. Or perhaps a more accurate term for it would be nightmare. There was no way she'd gone through the day of hell yesterday. It had to be some kind of terrible nightmare.

But here she was, in the Sheraton hotel room Rell had gotten for them after the shooting at his mom's house last night. He was fast asleep beside her with the blanket over his head.

Tirzah was asleep on the other bed, and Jah was in a bathrobe, pacing a tight circle next to the bed with his infant daughter cradled in his arms. He looked at Tamera and smiled.

"Merry Christmas," he said, in a low tone.

"Shit, it is Christmas, isn't it?" Tamera shook her head in disbelief. She was naked under the bathrobe she'd went to sleep wearing, because they all had sent their clothes down to the laundry before going to bed.

"I threw up about twenty times in a row," Jah said. "Man, I was so fucked up last night. Barely even got any sleep." He walked over and stopped at the foot of her and Rell's bed. "Did you see what happened at my momma's crib?"

Tamera nodded her head yes. She had been looking out Rell's bedroom window as the shooting took place. She had watched him run up on the guy in the hoodie and shoot him in the back. She had seen Tirzah blasting Jah's gun at the escaping car. And last but not least, she'd witnessed Rell use his boot to turn the man over before he shot the guy twice in the face.

"I was so fucked up," Jah said, "I barely remember the shit. I just know I love your sister now." He laughed. "She got down like a real rider out there, and I was off my square. I could've got whacked fuckin' around with that Henny. I'm done with that shit. From now on, I'm through drinkin'. If anything, I'll fuck with the Lean, but no more liquor."

Tamera's mouth was as dry as the desert, and she had a full bladder. She took her purse to the bathroom and brushed her teeth, then used the toilet and took a nice hot shower.

She was careful to set the ring on a folded towel before she stepped in the shower, and as soon as she was done showering, she put it back on and stared at it for a long moment, lost in its sparkling beauty. Then she checked her smartphone and gritted her teeth when she saw that the battery was dead. She hadn't brought her charger, and she was pretty sure Tirzah hadn't, either.

By the time she came out twenty minutes later, dressed only in her shirt and boy shorts, Tirzah was woke and holding the baby, and room service had just brought up a breakfast of cheese eggs, bacon, pancakes, waffles, and steak.

She sat down next to Rell and shook him awake. "Rell. Rell." She shook him some more. "Boy, get the hell up. Merry Christmas, y'all. Ain't no time to sleep. We got shit to do."

Reluctantly, Rell rolled over, squinting and looking around, from Tamera to Tirzah, from Tirzah to Jah, and back to Tamera again. His mouth stretched open in a mighty yawn.

Jah laughed. "Bruh, get'cho funky-breath havin' ass up, nigga. Eat some breakfast."

"For real," Tamera added, smiling as she leaned in to kiss him on the cheek. "And go brush your teeth, too."

"Fuck outta my face with that shit." Rell got up, looking grumpy, and went to the bathroom. When he returned a short while later he was shirtless, wearing only his boxers and jeans.

No one mentioned either of the shootings during breakfast, and afterward, Tirzah and Jah went to the bathroom together, leaving the baby with Tamera.

She didn't mind holding the cute little girl. Unlike most babies she'd held in the past, Dora was fairly quiet and full of smiles and giggles.

"I want a baby one day," she said, more to herself than to Rell.

He was counting through the pile of cash he'd gotten from collecting the rent yesterday. He'd left it on the nightstand overnight, along with his gun, his smartphone, some cigarillos, and a baggie full of Kush.

A moment later, stuffing the cash in his pocket, he turned to Tamera and lay back on the bed, checking his smartphone.

"Pops just gave me the address to send him the ring," he said.

Tamera sucked her teeth.

Rell grinned. "You do know that I didn't propose to you, right?"

She flipped up a middle finger without lifting her eyes from Dora's pretty face. "Shut up talking to me, Rell. Please. It's Christmas, and you all put me through hell yesterday. I'm trying to enjoy this day in peace."

"I was just saying...the ring ain't yours. Don't get too attached to it."

"Don't worry, I won't. I know better than to ever expect somebody to give me a ring."

"What's that supposed to mean?" Rell asked, putting a hand on her thigh.

"It means just what it sounds like. Nobody is going to marry me. Not the kind of man I want, at least. If anything, I'll have to settle for somebody I really don't wanna be with. No handsome man is going to be faithful in a relationship.

That's a fantasy. I'm grown enough to understand that now. Niggas these days only want a nut and a sandwich."

Tamera's tone of voice was hopeless and despondent. She had no faith in relationships. Kendrick and all the rest of her exes had proven time after time that no man was to be trusted. She'd pretty much given up on finding love.

"You sound dumb as fuck," Rell said, shaking his head as he continued to tap his thumbs on the screen of his smartphone. "You think I just run around puttin' my mouth on every bitch I meet? You know how many hoes I can have if I wanted 'em? A whole lot. My li'l bro be gettin' mad at me for turnin' down so much pussy. I want one woman. I wanna get married like my pops one day. Don't throw me in the same category as them fuck niggas you had in the past. Give me a chance to show you who I am first, 'cause you'll see that I'm nowhere near anything you've ever had."

Rell's kind words warmed Tamera's heart. She stared at him for a long while, wondering if he was telling her the truth or simply spitting game. He sure seemed like he was telling the truth. There had been no hesitation, no thought put into it, no sneaky smirk added to show that his true intentions were hidden away.

She looked at his phone and saw that he was on Facebook.

"My nigga Rev just shared this Fox 32 news link," he said. "Four dead, eight wounded overnight in North Lawndale shootings on Christmas Eve. One suspect in custody."

"Who's in custody?" Tamera asked.

"A nigga named Johnny B. One of Jah's li'l guys. He got caught running from a shooting on Millard last night, right when that shit was going down in the alley." Rell raised his head and locked eyes with Tamera. "You saw that shit, didn't you? You saw it from the window."

She nodded her head yes. "But I understand. You didn't really have a choice. Those were the same guys from the building."

"Yeah, and I think Tirzah whacked dude who came lookin' for her. They say he's dead, too. He was in that white car."

"That's crazy. Tirzah's not even that kind of girl."

"Nobody's a killer until they have to kill somebody. Can't blame her. Anybody would've done the same thing in that situation. I'm just mad that Jah was all drunk and shit. Nigga can't handle his liquor. That shit ain't cool. He could've died out there last night. Momma would've killed me about that shit."

"Well," Tamera said, "he wasn't hurt, so be grateful. You should be praying that the cops don't connect you to either of those shootings. That's what's most important."

Rell shrugged his shoulders and kept scrolling down his Facebook page.

The moans coming from the bathroom let Tamera know that Jah and Tirzah were up to no good. She sat the baby in the car seat at the foot of the bed, cuddled up next to Rell, and put her head on his chest.

The TV was on the news but it was muted, which was good for Tamera, because she didn't want to hear it. She was perfectly content with laying up with Rell to start her Christmas morning. He smelled so good, and the feel of his muscles were soothing. She put a fingertip on his abdomen and traced the lines of his six-pack, thinking about how her life would be if she spent the rest of her days with him. One thing he'd have to get rid of was the gunplay. She wasn't trying to lose him — not to the prison system, and certainly not to another shooting.

Her eyes fell on the ring for the fiftieth time since she'd awakened. Jesus Christ, it was beautiful. The huge diamond made her chest swell with hope. What if one day she did get proposed to by a man as handsome as Rell, with a ring as expensive as this one?

The thought brought back memories of her maternal grandmother, who had always said, "With God, all things are possible."

Maybe that was the answer. Maybe Tamera just needed to pray for things to go the way she wanted them to go. Maybe Rell really was a good man, and God was just waiting to hear a few prayers from Tamera to set the wheels of love in motion.

Tracing a heart on his abs, she shut her eyes and prayed in silence. *God, please forgive me for my sins. Please guide my heart in the right direction. Make this fling into something more, something special, something my mom can be proud of and that my sister can look up to. If it's in your will, I mean. I'd really appreciate it. In Jesus' name I pray, amen.*

She opened her eyes and canted her head upward so that she was looking up at Rell, who was still glued to his phone.

He must have sensed her stare.

"I'm serious," he said. "I wanna fuck with you and only you. I just hope you want the same thing."

"I do," Tamera replied, a little quicker than she'd intended. "I want something real, Rell. I'm tired of dealing with liars and cheaters. I deserve so much more than that."

"I agree. And I'm not a liar or a cheater, so you're good as far as that goes. Not saying I'm perfect, but I'm not a cheater. I like to eat pussy too much to be cheating. I want one woman who only wants one man. I'll be all the way good with that."

Tamera's smile grew wider and wider. She kissed his powerfully built chest and then giggled as Dora started laughing and throwing her hands in the air.

"She's with it, too," Tamera said, laughing as she sat up and tickled Dora's tummy. "Isn't that right, little momma? Your uncle is going to treat me right or we're going to beat him up. Yes, we are. Yes, we are!"

Rell kicked Tamera in the hip.

"Ouch." She rubbed the spot where his foot had struck her and gave his leg a slap. "Asshole."

"Come here," he said.

She crawled to him and sat on his lap. He put the smartphone down next to him and planted his hands on her ass, looking up at her with his tantalizing grin.

"So," he asked, "we're a couple? You're my lady now?"

"If that's what you want me to be."

"That's not the answer I wanted."

"Yes, Rell." She sighed. "I'm all yours."

His strong, rugged hands traveled up to her lower back, then his fingers slipped down into the rear of her boy shorts.

"Merry Christmas," he said.

"Merry Christmas to you, too, Rell. With your fine ass." She lowered her face to his and hovered for a moment before kissing his lips. "I prayed for this gift. Bet you didn't know that."

"I ain't much of a gift."

"Yeah, right. You must not have looked in the mirror this morning. You're the kind of man women dream of having. You're fine, in good shape, got a big thang down there. I couldn't have asked for more."

"You don't look too bad yourself. With this sexy ass body, and those lips. Mmm. Gimme another kiss."

She kissed him again, but this time the kiss lasted for a long while. He introduced his tongue to the kiss just seconds later, and she sucked it in her mouth, feeling his dick harden between her thighs. She reached down and massaged it through his jeans...until Dora began laughing again.

Tamera looked back at the cute little bundle of joy and laughed right along with her.

When Jah and Tirzah came out of the bathroom, they all packed up their things and left.

Chapter 28

There were no young hustlers standing on the corner of Homan and Douglas as Rell pulled up and parked in front of Tamera's car (someone had been kind enough to tape some plastic over the windows Stain had punched out).

The heavyset dark-skinned woman who'd refused to pay her rent early was standing inside the door, smoking a cigarette. Pieces of yellow crime scene tape littered the hallway floor behind her.

As Rell walked up and pulled the door open for Jah to enter with Dora in her car seat, the woman said, "The police was lookin' for yo' daddy. A nigga got killed in here yesterday. Everybody claimin' they ain't seen shit. That's a damned shame. I know that boy's momma. Somebody saw somethin'."

"It's a cold game," Rell replied.

Once they were on the second floor and out of the fat lady's earshot, Tamera said, "I can't stand that fat bitch. Always gossiping and sticking her nose in somebody else's business. Hoe, it's Christmas. If you don't get your ass in the house and open a gift or somethin'."

"I swear," Tirzah added, shaking her head. "Ol' nosy-ass Sandra. Always in somebody's business. Can't stand her."

Rell chuckled as they made it to Tamera and Tirzah's apartment. Both he and Jah gawked at the thick derrières their ladies possessed while Tirzah unlocked the door. The two sisters were carrying bags of food and other items Rell had purchased when he'd stopped at Walmart. He'd bought outfits and shoes for everyone, more than $1,700 worth. He'd also stopped by the liquor store for two more bottles of Hennessy, a case of Budweiser, and five packs of Backwoods cigarillos.

Tirzah was going to cook a turkey, macaroni and cheese, corn-bread, string beans, cabbage, and a whole chicken for their Christmas dinner.

"You call Momma yet?" Jah asked Rell.

"Nah, nope. I know she mad as ever."

"Hope she didn't talk to the law."

"She ain't gon' do that. Momma know the game. I left her $300, too. She ain't gon' do nothin' but get another bottle and enjoy her day off."

"Felicia all on my voicemail goin' ham, asking where her baby is and why the fuck I had Dora around when some shit like that went down, like I'm some kinda mu'fuckin' psychic or somethin' and could've guessed the shit. She say she comin' to get Dora."

Rell shook his head. They were walking into the girls' apartment. "Tell her you left the baby with me, then. We can't have her crazy ass comin' in here on bullshit with Tirzah."

"I know." Jah nodded.

Tamera was just closing the door when the one across the hall swung open. Looking back, Rell saw a pretty-faced yellow bone in multicolored pajamas standing there across the hall. He couldn't remember her name, but he remembered her handing him the rent money. She had her hair done perfectly, and there was a circular birthmark beneath her right eye.

"I'm the one who put the plastic on your car," she said to Tamera. "Girl, the cops was banging all on your door and shit. Martez from over on Millard got killed downstairs, and I guess they saw that glass all around Janky and wanted to see if you had anything to do with it. I don't know."

"Thanks, girl." Tamera crossed the hallway and hugged the girl, then turned to Rell and said, "This is Candy."

"I met him," Candy said, smiling and giving Rell a wave.

Rell took the bankroll out of his pocket, peeled off a hundred-dollar bill, and crossed the hall to hand it to Candy.

"Aw, you don't have to do this. Tamera's my girl."

"I know. I'm just being nice today. Merry Christmas." He smiled and walked back into the apartment.

Jah was pulling the two big bags of Kush out of Dora's diaper bag, and Tirzah was already in the kitchen preparing to get her chef on.

"Y'all got a scale?" Jah shouted to Tirzah.

"Yep. Under the coffee table," she shouted back.

"What about some baggies?"

Tirzah stuck her head out of the kitchen seconds later and tossed Jah a box of sandwich bags.

Rell took a seat next to his little brother and picked up the TV remote.

"I like her already, bruh," Jah said as he set up the digital scale on the table. "She thick, pretty, and she a hunnid. Got down wit'chu like that last night. You don't find bitches like her every day. I might stay with her."

"That's gon' be weird as hell if we end up havin' kids with 'em."

"Hell yeah. They gon' be double cousins." Jah let out a laugh and started bagging up ounces of Kush.

A minute or two later, Tamera came in and hopped right on Rell's lap.

"Oh, my God," Jah said. "You two niggas are too sentimental with that shit. Already in love. Didn't we just get all that out of our systems at the room?"

"Hater," Tamera said, dragging out the word until she was out of breath.

Rell rubbed her big soft ass and kissed her on the mouth. "Fuck that nigga, he ain't talkin' 'bout nothin'."

Tamera leaned forward so that her lips were right next to his ear and whispered, "You do know that you didn't pull out at your mom's house, right?"

"So what? I ain't never gon' pull out," he whispered back.

"I hope you know I plan on being married before I have kids."

"Well, we'll have to get married."

"I'm not playing, Rell."

"Neither am I. If you get pregnant with my baby, and you keep it solid with me, I ain't got no problem with that. I told you, that's what I want anyway."

Tamera lay her head on his shoulder and snuggled her face in the crook of his neck. He slid his hands all across her butt, feeling like this might be the best Christmas present he'd ever had.

His thoughts went to the ring.

He wondered if he'd one day end up putting one on Tamera's finger. He could definitely see himself with her. She was the kind of girl his parents would love to see him with, a sweet, beautiful Black woman with style and grace.

He thought of how she would look in a flowing white wedding dress. Then came the thought of who would be the man to walk her down the aisle.

"Where's your pops?" he asked. "Your real father."

"On the south side. He's a dope fiend. Don't worry, you won't be seeing or hearing from him. We haven't seen him in years."

"You don't want him around if you get married one day?"

She shook her head. "I've been good this long without him. And it's not like he'd show up. He'd be too high to even remember the wedding, and he'd probably steal the cake. I'm telling you, he's the worst father ever. He stole all our presents one Christmas. Then another time he broke in here when we were out of town and stole everything that wasn't nailed down. He took our clothes, our beds — he even took my curling iron. I was so pissed off, I swear. I'll never forget that feeling. I would never have him walk me down the aisle. Hell, I wouldn't trust him to walk me to my car. Nuh uh. I'd rather have your dad walk me down the aisle than mine."

Jah interrupted: "What was that? Did I miss something? 'Cause to me it sounded like y'all was over there whisperin' about gettin' married. Damn, bruh, was the pussy that good?"

"Shut the fuck up." Rell leaned over toward Jah and shoved his head to the side, and when Jah pulled back an arm to retaliate Tamera shielded Rell from the incoming blow.

"Don't touch my man, Jah," she said.

"Ain't this a bitch?" Jah said in a high-pitched tone. He laughed and shook his head. "That's a damn shame. You niggas in love already, ain't known each other twenty-four hours yet."

Tamera leaned back, smiling at Rell. "Baby, did you...hear something? Sounded like I just heard somebody hating. Did you hear it, too?"

"Nah, I didn't hear it. Hold on, let me listen a little closer." He cocked his head to the side.

Jah gave the lovebirds a middle finger and went back to bagging up the Kush.

Chapter 29

Apartment 2B was rented out to Barbara Ann Jameson, a 44-year-old devout crack addict and occasional confidential informant. She was toothless, and quite often foul-smelling.

All seven of her children lived out of state now. They had long ago grown tired of her abuse. She'd neglected them until they were old enough to leave, and today her mind state wasn't much different. She hated people just as much as she loved smoking crack, no matter if they were related to her or not. She was a taxi driver who'd been investigated several times for scamming her passengers out of extra money. Once her bills were paid, she put all the rest of her money toward her habit, and whenever she ran out of money, she tricked herself out to the young dealers for a fix.

Which is what she was doing now, squatting in front of Lil Zo with his dick stuffed halfway down her throat as he leaned back on the wall in her living room and smoked a cigarette.

Two of his friends — Chris and E — were standing off to the side of Barbara, waiting on their turns to have their dicks down her throat.

Barbara didn't mind. No, she didn't mind at all. She'd be getting a twenty-dollar bag of crack from each of them.

Just five minutes after she started sucking on him, Lil Zo gushed a load of cum in her mouth. She spit it out in the rag she had for that exact purpose, and after he gave her the $20 worth of crack, she went to work on E.

"Head gunfire," Zo said to Chris.

"You see that Impala back out there?" Chris said.

"Yeah, I saw it."

"Joe, we need to stick dude up," Chris suggested, reaching for Zo's cigarette. "He walkin' around with all that bread on him like that. Nigga askin' to get robbed."

"Man, I ain't on that." Zo shook his head and handed over the cigarette. "You see how Martez got done in fuckin' around. I'ma sell these jabs and take my ass home. If we gon' rob some mu'fuckas, it ain't gon' be them. And I think that's Jah's big brother. Jah with the shits, joe. We'll have to whack that nigga, 'cause he ain't goin' at gunpoint."

"Man...that was a fat-ass bankroll."

"It was, too. I saw that mu'fucka."

"I need that, bruh. I'll blow this pole about that." Chris took a small-caliber gun from under his black hoodie and shook the dreadlocks out from in front of his face.

"What is that gon' do?" Zo asked incredulously. "Nigga, you heard that bang. You saw Martez lost half his mu'fuckin' head, and Stain and Jamie got whacked last night. That li'l ass gun ain't gon' do shit. We gotta come better than that if we gon' pull it. You ain't about to get me clapped up out there. If we gon' come, we gon' come hard or we ain't comin' at all. Fuck that li'l-ass strap. We gotta go and get that .45 from yo' daddy. That'll do it."

Chris nodded thoughtfully. He was light-skinned like E, and his dreads were longer than Zo's. He was fifteen, the same age as Zo, and E was sixteen. He had on the same pair of Robin's Jeans that he'd worn for the past week, and his hoodie was no fresher. For as long as Zo had known him, he'd been the dummy of the crew, always coming up with plans that made no sense to anyone but him. But Zo had to admit that the idea of robbing the guy with the Impala didn't seem so dumb.

He guessed how much money had been in the huge pile of cash and figured it had to be at least $5,000. The guy's Impala was clean and new-looking. Whoever he was, there was one thing for certain, and that was he had good money, definitely more than either of them had.

"I'm telling you," Chris said, swiping the back of his wrist across his runny nose, "we don't need no big-ass strap, joe. A gun is a gun. This mu'fucka can kill like any gun can. I think we should do it. Soon as we catch that nigga walkin' out that door, I say we up on his ass and make him run that bread. Or it might be better to catch up with him later tonight. Stop bein' so fuckin' scary. Scared man ain't never made no money."

"That's a .25, bruh." Zo laughed and shook his head at the outrageous suggestion. "Look, though. If you wanna pull it, fuck it, we can pull it. But on chief, you better start blowin' if that nigga reach for his pistol. No hesitation. You ain't gon' get me killed out here. If we gon' do it we gon' do it the right way."

"Bet," Chris said, smiling and nodding like he always did when he got his way. He raised the gun and stared at it. "Got nine shots in this li'l mu'fucka. I'ma make every one of 'em count if I need to."

Chapter 30

When you wake up 'fore you brush your teeth
You grab your strap, nigga
Only time you get down on your knees
Shooting craps, nigga
Fuck what you heard, God blessin' all the trap niggas...

Nodding their heads to the beat of Future's "Trap Niggas", Rell and Jah were being entertained by the Lyon sisters, who were twerking in sweatpants as the music blared from their television.

Rell's eyes were crimson and low from the two Kush blunts he and Jah had smoked in Tirzah's bedroom (because Dora was in the living room). The girls had smoked their fair share of the loud as well, and though Jah wasn't drinking, everyone else was.

"Future went hard as fuck on this one, big bruh," Jah said. "That nigga done took over the rap game for trap niggas. Him and Yo Gotti. They still got it. Them other niggas fallin' off."

Rell only shrugged his shoulders. He was much more focused on the girls.

Tamera and Tirzah were going hard.

Their hands were currently on their knees, and they were bouncing their asses to the Future song, sometimes one cheek at a time.

According to Tirzah, the food was just about done. They were taking a break from the kitchen to have a bit of fun and excitement with Jah and Rell.

Rell thought that maybe they'd taken one too many shots of the cognac, and he was happy about it. Seeing Tamera pop and bounce her generous derrière was all the entertainment he needed for Christmas.

Of course he wanted more, though.

Which is the reason why he got up, wrapped his arms around her waist, and whispered in her ear:

"Let me talk to you in the back right quick. Won't take but a minute."

She turned and hopped up onto him, locking her legs around his waist. She pressed her lips to his, and when she pulled back, she was beaming.

"Yeah, right. Talk? Are you sure that's all you wanna do is talk? Because I honestly can't believe that for one second."

He shrugged his shoulders. "Believe what you wanna." He carried her away, half expecting Jah or Tirzah to voice their hateration, but he heard no objections as he took Tamera to her bedroom and dropped her on the bed.

Tamera's bedroom was crammed full of girly things. Teddy Bears, hair and nail products, heels and mirrors and framed posters of Drake, The Rock, and Tigger from Winnie the Pooh. The walls were pink like the carpet and the poster frames. All sorts of makeup littered the dresser, and there were Winnie the Pooh stickers on the mirror.

"This is crazy," Tamera said. "I'm already tipsy as fuck. I really need to stop drinking. For real, after New Year's Eve, I'm done with liquor. Weed, too."

Rell didn't care if she quit drinking or not. As long as she never stopped giving him the pussy he was fine with her every decision.

He moved on top of her, and they kissed for a long while. He put a hand in the fresh red sweatpants she'd put on earlier and found that she wasn't wearing underwear.

He dipped a finger into her and stirred it, biting down on the center of his lower lip and gazing wantonly into her eyes.

"This gotta be the wettest pussy I done ever had," he murmured.

She put on an appreciative smirk. "I do got that wet-wet. Fuck around and drown you in this thang."

"You ain't gon' drown shit."

"Keep playin'...mmm...and you gon' find out," Tamera said, moaning as his finger stimulated her lower region. "I hope you got a condom. We can't keep fuckin' without protection. I'm not about to be a single mother like everybody else around here. You gon' have to put a ring on it first before we go that far."

"I thought we just had this conversation."

"We did."

"Well?"

"You ain't put a ring on it yet, nigga. Just because I'm wearing your stepmother's ring does not make us engaged."

"Well, take it off, and I'll propose to you with it." Rell chuckled once and gave Tamera a kiss as she rolled her eyes.

Then he went down to the place he was hungry for and began kissing and licking at the crotch of her sweats.

"Damn, nigga," she said, "you gon' eat it through my sweats?"

"If that's what it takes," Rell said, and chuckled as he peeled off the sweatpants.

"You're a real life pussy monster, Rell. Does it taste that good to you?"

He nodded his head as he gave her clitoris a lick. "Yup. Like candy." Another lick. "Like peaches."

He found it kind of hard to believe that he was sucking on Tamera's pussy yet again. Usually he roasted the guys he sometimes hung out with for doing the same thing. Hopefully she was just as faithful and abstinent as she was claiming to be. Lord knows he'd have a fit if he found out he was licking on a thot.

The idea that he might be wrong about Tamera compelled him to limit the cunnilingus to just under two minutes. He stood up and whipped out his lengthy love muscle. Tamera stared at it in amazement, as if she hadn't seen it before.

"Condom," she said, but her tone wasn't too convincing, so Rell pushed in the bulbous head and then added a few more inches.

"Shut up," he said, grinning.

He kissed her lips to stop her from mentioning a condom again as he jammed in his entire length.

She gasped. Her heart-shaped lips parted to make way for a passionate moan.

Rell put his hands on her hips and rocked her with his deep, pounding thrusts. Unlike Erica, who sometimes exuded a foul stench during sex, Tamera smelled just as good as she tasted. Her beautiful brown face, full lips, and almond-shaped eyes held him spellbound.

He lowered his face to hers and hastened his thrusts.

"It's too...mmmmmm...big...too...Rell," she said between moans.

He felt her vaginal muscles contracting as she experienced an orgasm, but he didn't stop or even pause. The wet sounds grew louder. His thrusts became more intense. He kissed and sucked on the side of her neck and hammered in and out of her until he felt his scrotum tighten and lift up.

Once again, he ejaculated inside her. Short breaths blew from his nostrils as his dick twitched and spewed out his seed. He pressed his lips against her neck and kept them there for a long moment, until the last drops of semen had oozed out of him.

Then he collapsed onto the bed and lay down on his back. He stared at her ass as she got up from the bed. She snatched a couple of tissues out of a Kleenex box on the dresser and wiped them between her thighs.

"Hold on," she said, pulling on her sweatpants. "I'll get a wet towel."

Just as she left the bedroom, Rell's smartphone started ringing. It was with his 30-shot clip in one of the back pockets of his jeans, and his Glock handgun was in the other back pocket. He dug it out, saw that it was Big Man calling, and hesitantly answered.

"Yo, what it is, Pops?"

"Can you please explain to me why I got the cops calling me while I'm on vacation, talking about a murder? Who is the boy that got killed in my building? Can you tell me that much?"

Rell took a deep breath. "I don't know, Pops. I really don't. We had just left when it happened, so I ended up staying at a hotel room last night."

"You got the ring?"

As if on cue, Tamera came sashaying into the room at that very moment with her hand outstretched, studying the diamond. She tossed a damp facecloth to Rell, and he used it to clean the juices off his limp pole.

"Yeah," Rell said to Big Man, "I got it right here. Damn, you think I'ma steal it? Why you keep asking me about this ring?"

"Because your stepmother is being a bitch about the damned thing. You know I could care less. Don't know why I wasted all my money on it in the first place. Don't make no sense to pay that much for a ring. It ain't that much love in the world."

Rell chuckled and shook his head.

"Listen," Big Man sailed on, "I got somethin' nice for you and Jah for Christmas. Got a place for you to stay, and I got him a car. Well, I ain't bought a car just yet, but I'm giving him one. You can tell him. Ya asses is too old for surprises."

"You got us a house?"

"Ain't that what the hell I just said?"

"Where is it at?"

Big Man paused. "It ain't far from my building. As a matter of fact, it's right around the corner and up the way, on 15th and Trumbull. The house Lil Joseph used to live in with Denise."

"Is it ours to have?"

"That's what I said, ain't it? Damn, boy, clean out cha ears. Smokin' all that dope done made you deaf. Yeah, the place'll be in your name, but it's for the both of you. You can either give him the Impala and take the Escalade, or I'll give him the Escalade. Choice is yours—"

"I'll take the Escalade," Rell said quickly. His face lit up. This would be a joyous holiday after all.

He fixed his pants and belt, and almost as an afterthought, he pushed the clip in his gun.

"Find out what that shooting was about, if you can," Big Man said. "I don't need no war going on in my building. Susan's already saying she ain't coming back because of that call I got from the police."

"I'll see what I can find out, Pops."

"The keys to the new place are already on my keyring. It's the three keys with the red on 'em. 1530 South Trumbull Avenue is the address. And don't you dare move that ol' nasty girl Erica in with you. If it ain't a good woman, I don't want her in there, you hear me? There's two levels. You can stay downstairs. Let Jah get the upstairs. I'll get you some more furniture in there when I get home, or you can use some of the money I gave you. Give your brother a thousand dollars. I'll give it back to you. Merry Christmas. I gotta go and take this old hag to lunch. Call you later."

"Love you, Pops."

"I just bet you do. Go on over and check the place out. Hell, stay there if you need to. I think that guy getting killed might've just ended my stay in that building. Ain't no way Susan's coming back to it. Make sure you try and find out what went down with that murder. Talk to you later."

The call ended, and Rell looked up at Tamera, who seemed to be smiling because he was smiling. She had her hands planted on her wide hips, and her head was canted to the side.

"So," she asked, "you got an Escalade for Christmas? Is it the one Big Man drives?"

Rell nodded his head rapidly, wearing the biggest grin of the century. "Got a house, too. Probably gotta wait for my pops to get back in two weeks to get the truck, but it's mine. Me and Jah got a house, too. It's ours. We actually own it."

A look of uncertainty clouded Tamera's expression. She took off the ring and handed it to Rell.

He shook his head. "Nah, keep it on for now." He hesitated, gazing at her perfect brown visage. "I, uh...you wanna move in with me? You can, if you want. I know the house. It's a duplex. We'll be downstairs. Jah can stay upstairs. Or vice versa. Either way I'm—"

"Wait a minute, Rell." She moved forward and pressed an index finger to his lips. "Let's just let whatever happens happen. There's no need to rush into anything. Take it one day at a time."

"You're right. Come on, let me tell Jah." He held her waist in his hands and walked with her out of the bedroom.

They hadn't even made it to the kitchen when someone began banging on the front door.

Chapter 31

Webster "Lil Webb" Houston was a twenty-three-year-old mid-level drug-dealer with a big ego. Though he wasn't much of a tough guy, he had gotten into a number of shootouts with the local rival gangs (New Breeds and Gangster Disciples), and those incidents had earned him a certain level of respect in the North Lawndale neighborhood. Plus, his father had been the birdman back in the day. A lot of people believed that Webb had big money like his father used to, but the truth was he only had about $70,000, all of which had come from his own drug sales.

He had a few girls he was fucking, but there was nothing really official. No wifeys or main chicks.

The baddest one on his team was Tirzah Lyon, the curvaceous redbone who stayed in the apartment building on Homan and Douglas Boulevard. She was the closest thing he had to a main chick.

He'd just driven his Ford F150 truck back from Atlanta, Georgia with a kilo of cocaine stashed inside a spare tire. As soon as he walked in the door of his mom's house on 16th and Spaulding, his baby sister, Jessica, had filled him in about the fight Tirzah had with Sharon, and about Sharon's father, Stain, getting killed last night.

"They say Tirzah was all hugged up with some nigga on 13th right before Stain got killed over there, too," Jessica had said. "One nigga said it was Jah, another bitch said it was Johnny B. I don't know which, but what I do know is she's fuckin' around on you, big bro. We can't go for that kinda shit. Lemme know if you want me to whoop that trick. You know I won't hesitate to beat the brakes off her ass."

Webb knew Jah from seeing him around the hood. He also remembered going to Dvorak High School with Jah's older brother, Rell.

After putting up the brick of coke, Webb got back in his truck and drove to the building on Douglas. He had the type of truck that stuck out wherever he went, clean white paint with a glossy finish and 28-inch chrome rims. Everybody knew him, including Jah. The youngster couldn't possibly be bold enough to mess around with one of Webb's girls.

But sure enough, parked there at the curb in front of the building, was Rell's Impala. A thick-bodied girl with a reddish brown complexion and purple highlights in her hair was stomping her way up the porch stairs.

"If this li'l nigga Jah is in here fuckin' my bitch..." Webb had said as he got out of the truck. He followed the woman into the building and up the first flight of stairs. "I swear, if this li'l nigga Jah is fuckin' my bitch..." he repeated, grinding his teeth together.

The girl turned and looked at him. "Excuse me, what did you just say? Did you just say something about Jah fucking your bitch? I know you ain't talking about my Jah, as in my baby's daddy."

"Shit, I don't know. Move." Webb stepped around her and kept climbing the stairs.

The girl was right on his heels.

"Oh, hell yeah. Let me just follow you up these stairs, 'cause it sounds to me like somebody got Felicia fucked all the way up today."

Webb couldn't help but to laugh as the girl started muttering a prayer.

"Lord, please forgive me if I gotta fuck me a bitch up this Christmas morning. If this nigga got my baby around some stank-ass bitch, I'm bussing his head and hers too, and Lord,

I just ask that you forgive me on your day, because you know that this was not my intention when I left out my house."

On the third floor, Webb looked back at Felicia and said, "You a'ight, li'l mama?"

"Oh, I'm perfectly fine. You just lead the way." She was taking off her earrings. If not for the unfortunate circumstances, Webb would have definitely tried to get her number, or at least her Instagram name. She was a bad bitch, with thick thighs and a fat, round ass, just like Tirzah.

When he got to the door of Tirzah's apartment on the fourth floor, he gave it five hard pounds and then took a step aside and watched as Felicia put down her purse and cracked her knuckles.

Maybe Webb wouldn't have to get on Tirzah about fucking with Jah after all.

It seemed like Karma was going to take care of it for him.

Chapter 32

Jah glanced at Tirzah, who was fixing their plates. Then he moved his eyes to Rell.

"You told Felicia which apartment we was in?"

Rell shook his head no. "Nah. Hell nah. I ain't said shit. If anything, she'll go upstairs first."

"Might be that bitch Sharon," Tirzah said as she took off, walking to the door.

Tamera rushed off behind her sister, and Rell and Jah were seconds behind them.

Rell saw Tirzah pick up a baseball bat that was leaning against the wall just before she unlocked the door.

Instinctively, Rell and Jah grabbed their pistols as Tirzah swung open the door.

"Aw, shit," Jah said when he saw Felicia standing there in the hallway.

Tirzah gasped at the sight of Webb.

"Jah, where the fuck is my baby?" Felicia was pissed. "And which one of these hoes are you fucking?"

"Hoes?" Tamera said.

Webb reached in and grabbed Tirzah by the neck. He yanked her out into the hallway.

"You dumb-ass bitch! You just gon' fuck a nigga behind my—" Webb started.

Apparently, he hadn't seen the bat.

Tirzah raised the baseball bat and cracked Webb upside the head with it, and Tamera ran out the door and in one swift motion. She kicked Webb in the face and he doubled over.

The suddenness of the drama seemed to catch Felicia off guard. Her eyes flicked from Jah to the rumble in the hallway and back to Jah.

In those few seconds, Tirzah hit Webb twice more with the baseball bat, and Tamera caught him with several knees, kicks, and punches to the face. Blood sprayed onto the white stucco walls.

"Where is my baby?" Felicia snapped.

But then the situation became even more dramatic.

Webb stumbled away from Tamera and Tirzah and pulled a gun from inside his leather jacket.

"He got a gun!" Tamera shouted.

Felicia ran into the apartment.

Rell lifted his Glock and took aim at Webb just as Tirzah swung the bat with all of her might.

The very tip of the bat struck the side of Webb's head and knocked him unconscious. Tamera snatched up Webb's gun and gave him another kick to the face.

"Fuck nigga! Grab my sister like that again!" Tamera shouted as she and Tirzah dragged him to the stairs.

Rell couldn't believe his eyes.

Tirzah and Tamera used their feet to give Webb the push he needed to send him tumbling down the stairs. He landed almost exactly like Martez had landed yesterday. He got up a few moments later and rolled and flipped down yet another flight of stairs.

Felicia was in and out with Dora in less than sixty seconds. She cussed Jah out all the way down the stairs, though she wasn't in a fighting mood like she usually was. Rell suspected it was because she didn't want any parts of the Lyon sisters.

Rell decided to bring the party up to his father's apartment. He helped the girls carry all the food up to Big Man's kitchen, then went back with them so that they could grab their Christmas gifts from under the tree.

By the time they left with the gifts, Jah was coming back up the stairs.

"Dude just made it outside," Jah said with a dry chuckle. "He is fucked up, bruh. Bad. I mean real bad. That nigga leakin' everywhere out there."

Rell had no comment.

He and Jah helped the girls carry the rest of their things up to Big Man and Susan's apartment. He fed Life some cat food and milk, then sat at the kitchen table with Jah and the girls.

They ate in silence with their guns next to their plates.

What a Christmas this was turning out to be.

Chapter 33

"You say you want some Kush, right? I just got a text from a nigga who stay on 13th. He got ounces of Kush for $400. Two different kinds, too. Hawaiian and Dragon, whatever the hell that is. Want me to hit him up?"

PJ took a moment to respond. He was stretched out on the sofa in Shalonda's living room, rubbing his big belly and trying to forget the memory of his uncle Stain's dead body lying in the backseat of the car he'd abandoned on Independence Boulevard last night.

He'd just eaten a huge lunch. Shalonda's two daughters, Ebony and Nay Nay, were on the other side of the coffee table, playing with the many toys and electronic gadgets their mother and PJ had gotten them for Christmas.

"I need somethin' to blow," PJ said, shaking his head despondently. "Damn. Can't believe this shit. Niggas done murked my uncle. I told his ass to hurry up and air the crib out. He had the K. How in the fuck can you let a nigga get down on you with a pistol when you got a choppa?"

"Bullets kill. Bottom line," Shalonda said.

"Yeah, but Unc had the ups on 'em. We was supposed to off them niggas. It wasn't supposed to go how it went. I'm telling you, one of these days I'ma catch up with them niggas, and when I do it's a done deal. I'ma lay low for now. Let some time pass. Then I'ma pull up over there and wait for dude to come outside. As soon as he step out that door it's hammer time."

Shalonda giggled once. She rubbed PJ's belly for a long moment.

"Yeah," PJ said a minute later, "see what's up with that Kush smoke. I'll get a quad first, and if it's good I'll grab as much as he wanna sell. Just make sure you don't mention me.

Tell him it's for you. I don't want my name in nothin' right now."

"I got'chu, baby," Shalonda said, and dialed a number on her smartphone.

PJ eyed the kids. Ebony was ten years old and Nay Nay was eight. Their fathers had both been killed in gang violence, a fact that kind of bothered PJ. It made him feel more cautious than usual. He had a 9 millimeter pistol behind the pillow on the side of him, and there was already a round in the chamber.

If anything went down, he wouldn't be Shalonda's next dead lover.

He was glad that she put the call on speakerphone so that he could hear what was being said:

"Yo, what's up, Londa?"

"I want some o' that loud. How much for a quad?"

"Shit, a hunnid. This that certified loud smoke, too, on Neal. Both kinds."

"Damn, I can't get a deal? Let me get a quad for seventy-five. If it's good as you claim it is I'll be right back for a whole zip."

"Fuck it, I got'chu. Come on wit' it. This the only time you gettin' a deal, though. I gotta get this money back."

"Can you just bring it over here to me? You know I ain't got no car, and I am not about to walk all the way over there to 13th in all that snow."

The dealer hesitated. "Yeah. You gotta gimme a minute. Soon as I get done eatin', I'll drive over there."

"Okay, just call when you get here. I'll meet you out front."

"Yup."

Shalonda turned to PJ as the call ended. She was a brown-skinned girl with big boobs and the best head PJ ever had in his life. Most of the time he just let her suck his dick when they were alone together. Every time they were on the road in his SUV, she sucked him until his toes curled up in his shoes.

She leaned over him and gave him a kiss with her melons spilling over her black pajama top.

"We gon' get you some good Kush, daddy. Fuck them niggas who killed Stain. Sooner or later they'll get the same damn treatment. That's how it goes around here, anyway. The main people who get killed are the killers. Niggas ain't just going out like that. I know if a nigga killed one of mine, his ass would definitely get smoked right behind them."

"That's exactly what the fuck's gon' happen to the niggas who killed my uncle. I'ma smoke them niggas the same way. Fuck the bullshit."

PJ couldn't wait to get his sights on his uncle's killer. He'd been too busy ducking and speeding away to see the shooter's face, but he remembered seeing the young guy Stain had fought the other night. As long as he knew Jah's name and face, and where Jah lived, he had the upper hand.

Sooner or later, Jah would be just as dead as Stain, Martez, and Jamie.

Chapter 33

Once they were finished eating, Rell, Jah, Tamera, and Tirzah piled into the Impala and headed for the house on Trumbull, keeping their eyes peeled for the growing list of enemies they had gained over the past couple of days.

Rell had been in the house numerous times in the past. His friends the Earls had lived there for years. He couldn't count the number of nights he'd spent on the porch with the Earl family, drinking and smoking and cracking jokes.

"I hope the heat's on in there," Tamera said as they got out of the car.

"For real," Jah added.

There was a thin layer of ice on the stairs. Icicles hung from the sides of the roof. The windows on both floors had maroon curtains.

Rell's hands were already numb by the time he pushed the key into the front door and unlocked it.

"You sure Big Man said this our shit?" Jah asked.

"Yeah, nigga." Rell had yet to tell Jah about the car. He'd wait until he had the Escalade signed over to his name before making any rash decisions. No need in getting anyone's hopes up. Big Man was known to change his mind at a moment's notice.

Kicking the snow off the bottom of his boots, he pushed open the door. He unlocked the upstairs door first to let Jah in, then he went back downstairs and unlocked the door to his new home.

"Man, it already got furniture, bruh!" Jah shouted from upstairs just as Rell realized the same thing.

There were two gray leather sofas, two easy chairs, a glass-top coffee table, and a flat screen television in the living room. Both bedrooms had brand-new queen-sized beds and full bedroom sets. There was a washer and dryer in the laundry room, a ton of food in the pantry, and the refrigerator was fully stocked.

And yes, the heat was on. So was the water and cable.

"Boy," Tamera said, "all you need is some sheets and blankets in here and you're in the game."

Rell fell back onto one of the sofas and sighed. This was the kind of life he deserved. A nice home to call his own, an Escalade ESV, thousands of dollars in his pocket — life just didn't get any better than this.

Tamera took off her jacket and draped it over the arm of the sofa, then sauntered around the living room with her hands on her hips, looking at the sockets, and the floorboards, and the windowsills.

"Wish my daddy treated me and my sister to a house," she said.

"You better get the fuck away from those windows before Webb pull up out there and see you." Rell stared at his new lady friend's meaty buttocks as she walked aimlessly around the room. "I love seeing you in sweatpants, you know that?"

She turned to him and rolled her eyes. "I'm not worried about Webb's punk ass. Let him pull up if he wanna. I've never shot anybody but I won't hesitate to do it."

"You ain't gon' do shit."

"Well, let a nigga try me. Like Dej Loaf, nigga. I'ma kill his whole mu'fuckin' family. Fuck around and I'ma catch a body." She took the gun she'd taken from Webb off her hip and inspected it from all angles. "I bet he's so embarrassed. Got his ass beat and his gun taken by some girls."

"You better be careful. He ain't the one to play wit'. I heard he 'bout that action."

Tamera shrugged her shoulders. She crossed the room to Rell, set the gun on the coffee table, and straddled Rell's lap. He immediately moved his hands to her ass and gave it a squeeze.

"These past few days have been the craziest days of the year for me," she said. "I can still see that boy's head busting open when he took that bullet to the head in the hallway."

"I plead the fifth." Rell smirked.

"And the way you walked up on that nigga in the alley behind your mom's house—"

"I plead the fifth again."

"Shut up." She gave him a soft punch to the chest.

Just then, Jah and Tirzah came walking in wearing the widest of smiles.

"Man, I'm about to call Pops and thank him for about fifty minutes straight," Jah said. "Lemme see the car keys right quick, so I can go and drop off this Kush to this li'l thot on 16th."

Rell shook his head no. "After all this shit we done got into, you think I'ma let you go off somewhere by yourself? Hell no. If you goin' somewhere, I'm comin' wit'chu."

"I'll go with him," Tirzah volunteered.

"I don't need nobody to go with me," Jah said. "Long's I got this 32-shot stick in my strap I'm guwop. Throw me the keys, big bruh. I'll be right back."

Reluctantly, Rell tossed Jah the keys to his Impala and watched his little brother walk out the front door.

Tirzah stood there looking mildly upset.

"He'll be right back," Rell said.

Chapter 34

Jah turned on the Drake and Future mixtape, put his Ruger pistol on his lap, and rolled a blunt to smoke by himself, all the while glancing up and down Trumbull Avenue.

There was no one outside.

Apparently, everyone was inside, celebrating the holidays with their families.

He shifted into drive and pulled away from the curb, vibing to the beat of "Jumpman".

Jumpman, Jumpman, Jumpman, them boys up to something
They just spent like two or three weeks out the country
Them boys up to something they just not just bluffing
You don't have to call I hit my dance like Usher (Woo!)...

It didn't take long for Jah to make it to Shalonda's house on 16th and St. Louis, just a right at one corner and a left at the next. There were a few vehicles cruising along 16th Street, but not many. An older lady in a heavy green coat was hunched over with a plastic bag in hand, struggling against the cold air as she walked up 16th Street. She gave Jah a wave as he turned onto St. Louis and parked across the street from Shalonda's place.

He honked the horn twice and waited.

A couple of seconds passed before he saw Shalonda peek through the blinds on her living room window.

He waved for her to come on, then took the quarter-ounce of Kush out of his jacket's inside pocket. He'd weighed it up in his new bedroom at the house on Trumbull. With the bag, it weighed exactly 8.1 grams.

A chameleon-painted Tahoe on oversized rims that was parked two houses down suddenly caught his attention. He'd seen it somewhere else recently. He frowned thoughtfully as Shalonda came shuffling down her porch stairs bundled up in a full-length black leather coat. She was opening the passenger door when he remembered where he'd seen the Tahoe. It had been parked on Millard when he fought Stain. In fact, Stain had flung him against the Tahoe as they tussled.

"Here you go, Jah." Shalonda handed Jah a fifty, a twenty, and a five.

Still looking at the SUV, he reached over to her with the Kush. "You know whose Tahoe that is?" he asked.

"What? What Tahoe? Oh, that one down there? No, why?"

Jah shrugged. "Just askin'. Looks familiar."

"Well, I don't know. Never seen it until today. Is this shit any good? It better be worth my money."

Finally, Jah turned to Shalonda. She had the bag of Hawaiian Kush held up to her nose.

"Yeah, it smells and looks like the real deal," she said. "Thanks. I'll hit you later if I need some more. Be safe out here. You know it was like four people who got killed around here yesterday. Martez and Jamie got killed. Old dope fiend-ass Stain got killed."

"I heard about that shit." Jah nodded, turned down the volume on the music, and accepted the quick hug that he knew was coming. Shalonda always hugged him after he served her. He'd been selling weed to her for close to a year now.

This time, however, the hug didn't seem as genuine. It felt forced, like she really didn't want to touch him for some reason.

As he drove back to the house on Trumbull Avenue, he wondered what had gotten into Shalonda...and he also wondered who owned the colorfully-painted Chevy Tahoe.

To Be Continued...
Mobbed Up 2
Coming Soon

Submission Guideline

Submit the first three chapters of your completed manuscript to ldpsubmissions@gmail.com, subject line: Your book's title. The manuscript must be in a .doc file and sent as an attachment. Document should be in Times New Roman, double spaced and in size 12 font. Also, provide your synopsis and full contact information. If sending multiple submissions, they must each be in a separate email.

Have a story but no way to send it electronically? You can still submit to LDP/Ca$h Presents. Send in the first three chapters, written or typed, of your completed manuscript to:

LDP: Submissions Dept
Po Box 944
Stockbridge, Ga 30281

DO NOT send original manuscript. Must be a duplicate.

Provide your synopsis and a cover letter containing your full contact information.

Thanks for considering LDP and Ca$h Presents.

Coming Soon from Lock Down Publications/Ca$h Presents

BOW DOWN TO MY GANGSTA

By **Ca$h**

TORN BETWEEN TWO

By **Coffee**

BLOOD OF A BOSS **VI**

SHADOWS OF THE GAME II

TRAP BASTARD II

By **Askari**

LOYAL TO THE GAME **IV**

By **T.J. & Jelissa**

IF LOVING YOU IS WRONG… **III**

By **Jelissa**

TRUE SAVAGE **VIII**

MIDNIGHT CARTEL IV

DOPE BOY MAGIC IV

CITY OF KINGZ III

By **Chris Green**

BLAST FOR ME **III**

A SAVAGE DOPEBOY III

CUTTHROAT MAFIA III

DUFFLE BAG CARTEL VI

HEARTLESS GOON VI

By **Ghost**

A HUSTLER'S DECEIT III

KILL ZONE **II**

BAE BELONGS TO ME III
A DOPE BOY'S QUEEN III
By **Aryanna**
COKE KINGS V
KING OF THE TRAP III
By **T.J. Edwards**
GORILLAZ IN THE BAY V
3X KRAZY III
De'Kari
THE STREETS ARE CALLING II
Duquie Wilson
KINGPIN KILLAZ IV
STREET KINGS III
PAID IN BLOOD III
CARTEL KILLAZ IV
DOPE GODS III
Hood Rich
SINS OF A HUSTLA II
ASAD
KINGZ OF THE GAME VI
Playa Ray
SLAUGHTER GANG IV
RUTHLESS HEART IV
By Willie Slaughter
FUK SHYT II
By Blakk Diamond
TRAP QUEEN

RICH $AVAGE II

By Troublesome

YAYO V

GHOST MOB II

Stilloan Robinson

CREAM III

By Yolanda Moore

SON OF A DOPE FIEND III

HEAVEN GOT A GHETTO II

By Renta

FOREVER GANGSTA II

GLOCKS ON SATIN SHEETS III

By Adrian Dulan

LOYALTY AIN'T PROMISED III

By Keith Williams

THE PRICE YOU PAY FOR LOVE III

By Destiny Skai

I'M NOTHING WITHOUT HIS LOVE II

SINS OF A THUG II

TO THE THUG I LOVED BEFORE II

By Monet Dragun

LIFE OF A SAVAGE IV

MURDA SEASON IV

GANGLAND CARTEL IV

CHI'RAQ GANGSTAS IV

KILLERS ON ELM STREET IV

JACK BOYZ N DA BRONX II

A DOPEBOY'S DREAM II

By **Romell Tukes**

QUIET MONEY IV

EXTENDED CLIP III

THUG LIFE IV

By **Trai'Quan**

THE STREETS MADE ME III

By **Larry D. Wright**

IF YOU CROSS ME ONCE II

ANGEL III

By **Anthony Fields**

FRIEND OR FOE III

By **Mimi**

SAVAGE STORMS III

By **Meesha**

BLOOD ON THE MONEY III

By J-Blunt

THE STREETS WILL NEVER CLOSE II

By K'ajji

NIGHTMARES OF A HUSTLA III

By King Dream

IN THE ARM OF HIS BOSS

By Jamila

HARD AND RUTHLESS III

MOB TOWN 251 II

By Von Diesel

LEVELS TO THIS SHYT II

By Ah'Million

MOB TIES III

By SayNoMore

BODYMORE MURDERLAND III

By Delmont Player

THE LAST OF THE OGS III

Tranay Adams

FOR THE LOVE OF A BOSS II

By C. D. Blue

MOBBED UP II

By King Rio

Available Now

RESTRAINING ORDER **I & II**

By **CA$H & Coffee**

LOVE KNOWS NO BOUNDARIES **I II & III**

By **Coffee**

RAISED AS A GOON I, II, III & IV

BRED BY THE SLUMS I, II, III

BLAST FOR ME I & II

ROTTEN TO THE CORE I II III

A BRONX TALE I, II, III

DUFFLE BAG CARTEL I II III IV V

HEARTLESS GOON I II III IV V

A SAVAGE DOPEBOY I II

DRUG LORDS I II III

CUTTHROAT MAFIA I II

By **Ghost**

LAY IT DOWN **I & II**

LAST OF A DYING BREED I II

BLOOD STAINS OF A SHOTTA I & II III

By **Jamaica**

LOYAL TO THE GAME I II III

LIFE OF SIN I, II III

By **TJ & Jelissa**

BLOODY COMMAS I & II

SKI MASK CARTEL I II & III

KING OF NEW YORK I II,III IV V

RISE TO POWER I II III

COKE KINGS I II III IV

BORN HEARTLESS I II III IV

KING OF THE TRAP I II

By **T.J. Edwards**

IF LOVING HIM IS WRONG…I & II

LOVE ME EVEN WHEN IT HURTS I II III

By **Jelissa**

WHEN THE STREETS CLAP BACK I & II III

THE HEART OF A SAVAGE I II III

By **Jibril Williams**

A DISTINGUISHED THUG STOLE MY HEART I II & III

LOVE SHOULDN'T HURT I II III IV

RENEGADE BOYS I II III IV

PAID IN KARMA I II III

SAVAGE STORMS I II

By **Meesha**

A GANGSTER'S CODE I &, II III

A GANGSTER'S SYN I II III

THE SAVAGE LIFE I II III

CHAINED TO THE STREETS I II III

BLOOD ON THE MONEY I II

By **J-Blunt**

PUSH IT TO THE LIMIT

By **Bre' Hayes**

BLOOD OF A BOSS **I, II, III, IV, V**

SHADOWS OF THE GAME

TRAP BASTARD

By **Askari**

THE STREETS BLEED MURDER **I, II & III**

THE HEART OF A GANGSTA I II& III

By **Jerry Jackson**

CUM FOR ME I II III IV V VI VII

An **LDP Erotica Collaboration**

BRIDE OF A HUSTLA **I II & II**

THE FETTI GIRLS **I, II& III**

CORRUPTED BY A GANGSTA I, II III, IV

BLINDED BY HIS LOVE

THE PRICE YOU PAY FOR LOVE I II

DOPE GIRL MAGIC I II III

By **Destiny Skai**

WHEN A GOOD GIRL GOES BAD

By **Adrienne**

THE COST OF LOYALTY I II III

By Kweli

A GANGSTER'S REVENGE **I II III & IV**

THE BOSS MAN'S DAUGHTERS I II III IV V

A SAVAGE LOVE **I & II**

BAE BELONGS TO ME I II

A HUSTLER'S DECEIT I, II, III

WHAT BAD BITCHES DO I, II, III

SOUL OF A MONSTER I II III

KILL ZONE

A DOPE BOY'S QUEEN I II

By **Aryanna**

A KINGPIN'S AMBITON

A KINGPIN'S AMBITION **II**

I MURDER FOR THE DOUGH

By **Ambitious**

TRUE SAVAGE I II III IV V VI VII

DOPE BOY MAGIC I, II, III

MIDNIGHT CARTEL I II III

CITY OF KINGZ I II

By **Chris Green**

A DOPEBOY'S PRAYER

By **Eddie "Wolf" Lee**

THE KING CARTEL **I, II & III**

By **Frank Gresham**

THESE NIGGAS AIN'T LOYAL **I, II & III**

By **Nikki Tee**

GANGSTA SHYT **I II &III**

By **CATO**

THE ULTIMATE BETRAYAL

By **Phoenix**

BOSS'N UP **I , II & III**

By **Royal Nicole**

I LOVE YOU TO DEATH

By Destiny J

I RIDE FOR MY HITTA

I STILL RIDE FOR MY HITTA

By **Misty Holt**

LOVE & CHASIN' PAPER

By **Qay Crockett**

TO DIE IN VAIN

SINS OF A HUSTLA

By **ASAD**

BROOKLYN HUSTLAZ

By **Boogsy Morina**

BROOKLYN ON LOCK I & II

By **Sonovia**

GANGSTA CITY

By **Teddy Duke**

A DRUG KING AND HIS DIAMOND I & II III

A DOPEMAN'S RICHES

HER MAN, MINE'S TOO I, II

CASH MONEY HO'S

THE WIFEY I USED TO BE I II

By Nicole Goosby

TRAPHOUSE KING **I II & III**

KINGPIN KILLAZ I II III

STREET KINGS I II

PAID IN BLOOD **I II**

CARTEL KILLAZ I II III

DOPE GODS I II

By **Hood Rich**

LIPSTICK KILLAH **I, II, III**

CRIME OF PASSION I II & III

FRIEND OR FOE I II

By **Mimi**

STEADY MOBBN' **I, II, III**

THE STREETS STAINED MY SOUL I II

By **Marcellus Allen**

WHO SHOT YA **I, II, III**

SON OF A DOPE FIEND I II

HEAVEN GOT A GHETTO

Renta

GORILLAZ IN THE BAY **I II III IV**

TEARS OF A GANGSTA I II

3X KRAZY I II

DE'KARI

TRIGGADALE I II III

Elijah R. Freeman

GOD BLESS THE TRAPPERS I, II, III

THESE SCANDALOUS STREETS I, II, III

FEAR MY GANGSTA I, II, III IV, V

THESE STREETS DON'T LOVE NOBODY I, II

BURY ME A G I, II, III, IV, V

A GANGSTA'S EMPIRE I, II, III, IV

THE DOPEMAN'S BODYGAURD I II

THE REALEST KILLAZ I II III

THE LAST OF THE OGS I II

Tranay Adams

THE STREETS ARE CALLING

Duquie Wilson

MARRIED TO A BOSS... I II III

By Destiny Skai & Chris Green

KINGZ OF THE GAME I II III IV V

Playa Ray

SLAUGHTER GANG I II III

RUTHLESS HEART I II III

By Willie Slaughter

FUK SHYT

By Blakk Diamond

DON'T F#CK WITH MY HEART I II

By Linnea

ADDICTED TO THE DRAMA I II III

IN THE ARM OF HIS BOSS II

By Jamila

YAYO I II III IV

A SHOOTER'S AMBITION I II

By S. Allen

TRAP GOD I II III

RICH $AVAGE

By Troublesome

FOREVER GANGSTA

GLOCKS ON SATIN SHEETS I II

By Adrian Dulan

TOE TAGZ I II III

LEVELS TO THIS SHYT

By Ah'Million

KINGPIN DREAMS I II III

By Paper Boi Rari

CONFESSIONS OF A GANGSTA I II III

By Nicholas Lock

I'M NOTHING WITHOUT HIS LOVE

SINS OF A THUG

TO THE THUG I LOVED BEFORE

By Monet Dragun

CAUGHT UP IN THE LIFE I II III

By Robert Baptiste

NEW TO THE GAME I II III

MONEY, MURDER & MEMORIES I II III

By Malik D. Rice

LIFE OF A SAVAGE I II III

A GANGSTA'S QUR'AN I II III

MURDA SEASON I II III

GANGLAND CARTEL I II III

CHI'RAQ GANGSTAS I II III

KILLERS ON ELM STREET I II III

JACK BOYZ N DA BRONX

A DOPEBOY'S DREAM

By **Romell Tukes**

LOYALTY AIN'T PROMISED I II

By Keith Williams

QUIET MONEY I II III

THUG LIFE I II III

EXTENDED CLIP I II

By **Trai'Quan**

THE STREETS MADE ME I II

By **Larry D. Wright**

THE ULTIMATE SACRIFICE I, II, III, IV, V, VI

KHADIFI

IF YOU CROSS ME ONCE

ANGEL I II

By **Anthony Fields**

THE LIFE OF A HOOD STAR

By Ca$h & Rashia Wilson

THE STREETS WILL NEVER CLOSE

By K'ajji

CREAM I II

By Yolanda Moore

NIGHTMARES OF A HUSTLA I II

By King Dream

CONCRETE KILLA I II

By Kingpen

HARD AND RUTHLESS I II

MOB TOWN 251

By Von Diesel

GHOST MOB II

Stilloan Robinson

MOB TIES I II

By SayNoMore

BODYMORE MURDERLAND I II

By Delmont Player

FOR THE LOVE OF A BOSS

By C. D. Blue

MOBBED UP

By King Rio

BOOKS BY LDP'S CEO, CA$H

TRUST IN NO MAN

TRUST IN NO MAN 2

TRUST IN NO MAN 3

BONDED BY BLOOD

SHORTY GOT A THUG

THUGS CRY

THUGS CRY 2

THUGS CRY 3

TRUST NO BITCH

TRUST NO BITCH 2

TRUST NO BITCH 3

TIL MY CASKET DROPS

RESTRAINING ORDER

RESTRAINING ORDER 2

IN LOVE WITH A CONVICT

LIFE OF A HOOD STAR